KAROLINA PAVLOVA

A DOUBLE LIFE

Translated and with an introduction by

BARBARA HELDT

Barbary Coast Books

First edition published by Ardis, Ann Arbor, 1978.
Second edition published by Barbary Coast Books, 1986.
Third printing, with corrections, 1990.

PRINTED IN U.S.A.

Barbary Coast Books
P.O. Box 3645
Oakland, California 94609

ISBN 0-936041-01-3 (pbk.)

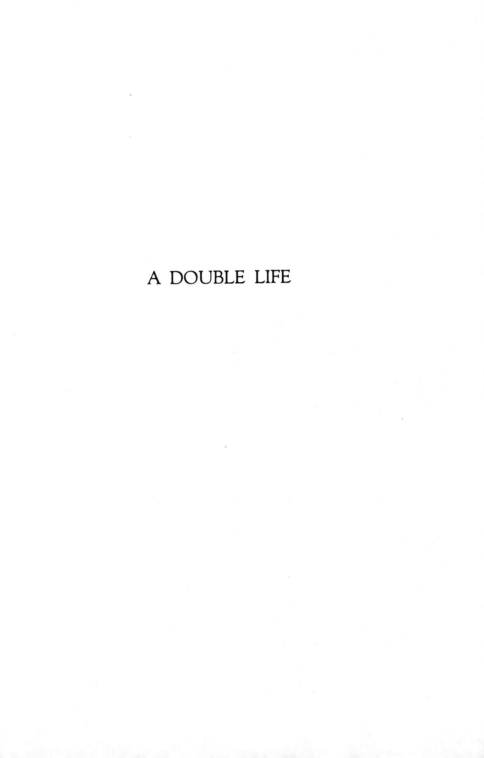

A DOUBLE LIFE

Karolina Pavlova: The Woman Poet and the Double Life

I

In the nineteenth century, when its literature equalled that written at any place at any time in history, Russia had no great woman writer—no Sappho, no Ono no Komachi or Murasaki Shikibu, no Madame de Staël or George Sand, no Jane Austen or George Eliot—or so we might say when surveying the best-known works of the age. And it would be almost true, but not quite.

Karolina Pavlova, born Karolina Karlovna Jaenisch in Yaroslavl in 1807, died in Dresden in 1893 after having lived outside Russia for four decades. She had abandoned her native country not because of Tsarist oppression but because of hostile criticism of her poetry and her personal life. She died without friends, without family, without money, without renown (not a single Russian newspaper gave her an obituary),[1] but with an unyielding dedication to what she called her "holy craft," which had produced a body of fine literary works, largely poetic.

In 1848, when she had completed her only novel, *A Double Life*, Pavlova was not only devoted to art but also enjoyed the other, more transient pleasures like love, friendship and respect, which she was to lose later on. To judge from the irony that pervades her otherwise romantic description in this book of a young girl who has everything, even at that time Karolina Pavlova had come to expect little from the world beyond what her own talents and personality could bring to it. The theme of conflict between

i

poet and society had informed the works of the great lyric poets who were her predecessors, Pushkin and Lermontov. Pavlova returned to this theme again and again, translating her emotion into verse of abstract classical precision which her detractors called cold, heartless, and remote from the "real" problems of life. Even when there was admiration for her poetry, it was mixed with ridicule of her. Thus a letter of her fellow-poet Iazykov in 1832[2] contains hints that this extraordinary phenomenon, a woman poet, was somehow ridiculous when reciting her poetry, as was then the custom. In this way was engendered a more subtle conflict than that of poet versus society—that of woman-poet versus society and, ultimately, of woman versus poet within Pavlova herself.

As much as any woman of her time could in Russia, Pavlova lived in a man's world. Her father, Karl Jaenisch, was professor of physics and chemistry at the School of Medicine and Surgery in Moscow; many university professors in Russia were, like him, of German origin. Jaenisch adored his daughter and saw to it that she received a superb education at home, the only place in Russia where a woman could get a higher education (Moscow University was not officially open to women until 1876). Her first romantic love was the great Polish poet Adam Mickiewicz who tutored her in Polish (she already knew, in addition to Russian, French, German, Spanish, Italian, Swedish and Dutch) and was stunned by her literary talents. In the late 1820s Karolina Jaenisch was already attending the important literary gatherings in Moscow, translating poetry, and writing her own in German and French. In 1833 her first book appeared—translations of Russian poets into German, called *Das Nordlicht*.

In December of 1836 she married Nikolai Pavlov, a minor figure in the world of letters whose talent soon ran dry. Pavlov's friend Chicherin wrote in his memoirs that Pavlov confessed to having married Karolina for her money—

"a social misdemeanor," Chicherin says, "that is quite usual and looked upon with indulgence."[3]

On Thursdays in their Moscow house from 1839 to 1844, the leading figures of the day attended the Pavlov's literary salon.[4] Poets would read aloud from their latest works and the exponents of the two social philosophies of the age, the Slavophiles and the Westernizers, would gather for sharp debates until their mutual hostility grew too great for social gatherings. The Pavlovs had a son named Ippolit who recalled how his mother would often retire from her large and noisy household and compose her verses by saying them aloud, walking back and forth in her room, repeating, rearranging and modifying words and phrases.[5]

An alien figure both because she was perceived as being "German" and because she was a woman-poet, Pavlova lived above all for her art. The recurrent theme in her relationships with all her famous contemporaries is her need through their friendship to confirm her view of herself as a poet. In poetry dedicated to them, she constantly reiterates what she wrote to Baratynsky in 1842: "You have called me poet, / Liking my careless verse; / And I, warmed by your light, / Believed, then, in myself."

But circumstances of her life contrived to undermine this belief. If Pavlov married Karolina for her money, he soon began to gamble it away, sometimes at the rate of ten to fifteen thousand rubles an evening. Friends noticed that as her literary fame increased and his declined, he grew jealous: "Soon her poetry will be read more than his short stories. It seems he fears this."[6] Pavlov set up a separate household with a younger cousin of his wife whom Karolina had taken in and helped support.

The loneliness of Pavlova's position was greatly intensified by the fact that, despite the long list of famous men among her acquaintances, most of her male contemporaries disliked her intensely and interpreted her shaky pride as haughtiness and her love of poetry as theatrical posing. As a Soviet scholar has written: "The ironic references to Karolina Jaenisch are as frequent as the well-wishing ones, if not more frequent, and the latter in their tone . . . invariably include a shade of irony and mockery. The number of epigrams aimed at Jaenisch appear not less in number than the number of album verses full of praise and ecstasy."[7] To live only for art seemed to many a monstrous thing in a woman, or at best something to be indulgently patronized.

From I.I. Panaev, the powerful editor and minor writer and publicist, comes the most consistently unfavorable picture of her. He claims to have felt "timidity" in her presence:

> Before me was a tall, extremely thin lady, stern and majestic in appearance. . . . In her pose, in her glance was something affected, rhetorical. She stopped between two marble columns, with dignity she inclined her head slightly at my bow and then extended her hand to me with the majesty of a theatrical empress. . . . Within five minutes I learned from Mrs. Pavlov that she had received much attention from Alexander (von) Humboldt and Goethe—and the latter had written some lines to her in her album . . . then the album with these precious pages was brought forth. . . . Within a quarter of an hour Karolina Karlovna was declaiming to me some verses translated by her from German and English. . . .[8]

By sharing her work in this manner with someone whom she respected, Pavlova may have thought she was acting the way a poet was supposed to act, that she was *being a poet*; but as a woman she obviously was not entitled to act this way. Panaev also relates that Pavlova treated her husband rudely, as well she might have, considering that by then Nikolai was gambling away her entire estate. Panaev, too, seems to be responsible for the glib slanders of Pavlova's verse which followed naturally from his dislike of her person. Once when Granovsky had begun to praise her poetry, Panaev set him straight by reading a parody of Pavlova and then, so he claims, Granovsky had nothing further to do with her. Panaev's poem, like all his "parodies," is actually a satire directing itself to Pavlova's person rather than an attempt to imitate parodically the qualities of her verse. Another and more genuine parody of Pavlova, called "My Disillusionment," by another critic on the left, the poet Nekrasov, bemoans the possibility that women might want to give up jelly-boiling and pickle-making for philosophy and literature. One can only regret that Nekrasov, whose sympathy for fallen women, as the prostitutes of the time were romantically called, was often expressed in his poetry, was incapable of extending a similar sympathy to women of letters.

D.V. Grigorovich, in his memoirs, repeats a common criticism of Pavlova's poetry which, since it was untrue, seemed to stem from both ideological and personal dislike. He says that when they were introduced "not half an hour had gone by after the customary courtesies but she was already reading to me and the two or three other people sitting there her verses, which are distinguished more by the beautiful sounds of the words than the poetic content."[9] This criticism of her verse, that it subordinated sense to sound, reflects a common charge made by poets and critics of utilitarian persuasion against those of either the Slavophile or the art for art's sake philosophy. Panaev and *The Contemporary* were Pavlova's opponents in an intellectually polarized Russia, and she in turn condemned the utilitarians as "cold minds" (in her "Poslanie I.S. Aksakovu" of 1846).

Even Pavlova's literary friends wrote, if not articles and memoirs, then private letters condemning her as a woman. The Slavophiles appreciated Pavlova as a poet not only for the nationalist content of some of her verses but also for making Russian poetry known abroad through her translations. Yet when Pavlova finally took matters in hand and initiated proceedings which led to her husband's arrest after he had in secret mortgaged her property, even her closest friends turned against her. She could not have foreseen that Pavlov's reputation as a liberal would bring about a search of his library which contained some censored books; he was jailed and sentenced to a ten-month exile in Perm. He was later pardoned by the authorities and returned to live with his wife's cousin, but their friends never forgave Pavlova.

During the early months of 1853 Pavlova wrote nothing. She left for Petersburg, where her father died in a cholera epidemic. Trying to avoid contagion, she left without attending his burial, and a new scandal arose because of her treatment of the dead man. In May of 1853 she settled in Dorpat with her son and mother. In the midst of her distress she met a law student named Boris Utin who, twenty-five years younger than she, was the profoundest love of her life. Her long poetic silence was broken in January 1854 with a poem which celebrated their meeting and the rare relationship of equals Pavlova needed to have with men. In contains a double tension. The first is one of two people communicating while at the same time participating in society games (Pavlova does not indulge in Byronic rejection of society; she describes the even more difficult triumph of feeling within its context). The second tension is that between two people themselves as they experience, fight and resolve a complete sexual and spiritual attraction. Initially as enemies and finally as brothers, they are always equals.

> Strange, the way we met. In a drawing-room circle
> With its empty conversation,

Almost furtively, not knowing one another,
  We guessed at our kinship.

And we realized our souls' likeness
  Not by passionate words tumbling at
                random from our lips,
But by mind answering mind,
  And the gleam of hidden thoughts.

Diligently absorbed by modish nonsense,
  Uttering witty remarks,
We suddenly looked at each other
  With a curious, attentive glance,

And each of us, successfully fooling them all
  With our chatter and joking,
Heard in the other the arrogant, terrible
  Laughter of the Spartan boy.

And, meeting, we did not try to find
  In the other's soul an echo of our own.
All evening the two of us spoke stiffly
  Locking up our sadness.

Not knowing whether we would meet again,
  Meeting unexpectedly that evening,
With strange truthfulness, cruelly, sternly,
  We waged war until morning.

Abusing every habitual notion,
  Like foe with merciless foe,
Silently and firmly, like brothers,
  Later we shook hands.

In February 1854, Pavlova's son Ippolit went back to
Russia to live with his father and attend university the

following year. Pavlova settled in Dresden in 1858 and remained there for the rest of her life, in exile from the language in which she wrote, from the poetic tradition she had admirably continued, from the country and the city she loved, scorned by the prominent people she had known best, who were at their best her literary peers.

Pavlova continued writing. She reminds one of George Sand, who worked eight hours a day no matter what the emotional turmoil in her life. One of Pavlova's former literary friends, Ivan Aksakov, visited her in 1860 in Dresden, where she was living on a strict budget. Aksakov chose to give a negative interpretation to what might have been a refusal to let her grim life drag her under:

> She, of course, was extremely happy to see me, but within ten minutes, even less, was already reading her verse to me. . . . She is completely bold, merry, happy, self-satisfied to a high degree, and occupied only with herself. This is such a curious psychological subject, it should be studied. It would seem that the catastrophe which has reached her, a true misfortune experienced by her, the separation from her son, loss of her place in society, name and wealth, her poverty, the necessity of living by her labors—all this, it would seem, would strongly shake a person, leave profound traces on him . . . nothing of the sort, she is the same as always, has not changed at all except that she has grown older and everything that has happened to her has only served as material for her verses. . . . It's astonishing! In this woman filled with talent everything is rubbish—there is nothing serious, profound, true and sincere—at bottom there is an awful heartlessness, a dullness, a lack of development. Her sincerity of soul exists only in the form of art, all of it has gone into poetry, into verse, instead of feeling there is a sort of external exaltation. You feel that, of course,

she herself does not realize that she loves no one, that for her nothing is cherished, dear, holy. . . .[10]

Aksakov says she is "poisoned by Art." Strength of character thus becomes weakness or disease.

The riddle of Pavlova's nature that Aksakov sets up seems to be easily solvable. Pavlova's quickness to declaim her verses, her strident living for her craft alone which is so emphatically noticed by all the sources quoted, can be seen as another kind of attempt to prove to herself that despite her womanhood she was indeed a serious poet, not a mere salon hostess, a poetry-writing lady, as most of even her more gifted female predecessors in Russia had been.

At times the effort of being both poet and woman led to a split between Pavlova's poetic philosophy and the philosophy of life, a double life of the spirit. In the same letter, Aksakov writes of Pavlova: "She will tell you that she no longer believes in human friendship—and it's all nonsense, and within five minutes in her poetry, excellent poetry, she boasts that she has preserved her faith in friendship and in people."

One wonders if a man thus dedicated to his craft would have to endure similar constant accusations of contradictory, almost hypocritical emotions or "dryness of heart," as Chicherin put it. In any case, Pavlova could not help being affected by these criticisms and sometimes showed it. Her own writings give quite a different picture from that of a woman sure of her art and cold to life. We have a report from Ivan Aksakov's sister, quoted in one of his 1860 letters, that "Karolina Karlovna is upset and says that poetry is not a serious occupation and she is looking for a serious occupation." Aksakov's sister tells him to reassure Pavlova that "the chief business of her life is the education of her son and her maternal calling" and since these are assured, "she can without pangs of conscience devote herself to occupations not serious."[11] One can imagine how consoling this advice of a typical, well-meaning woman of her circle must have been to Pavlova.

The harsh criticism of her poetry in *The Contemporary* led Pavlova to write Panaev a long, rambling letter full of deprecation both of her sex and of her art. However grand their tone, the following words show that Pavlova's doubts and hesitations always took the form of questioning herself as a *woman* poet:

> It is said that the chief content of a woman's letter is in the postscript: I give you new proof of the truth of this pronouncement; only at the end of my letter do I decide to utter what is foremost in my heart, that your criticisms cut me to the quick. I do not repudiate my sex and have not conquered its weaknesses; whatever you may say, a woman-poet always remains more woman than poet and authorial egotism in her is weaker than female egotism. . . . I have never wished nor tried to make myself an author; this necessity that exists in me for better or for worse, this calling I keep in check as much as I can. . . .[12]

Thus Pavlova tries to defend her innocence; she is guilty only of the petty vanity of women, not the colossal vanity of a woman who wants to be a poet. She apologizes for her talent to the man who edited the most powerful journal of the time, but, as we have seen, in vain.

In exile Pavlova came to view life as a challenge to survive. As she wrote to Olga Kireeva from Dresden on July 22, 1860, when alone and beset by financial difficulties, "I am occupied with the contemplation of an interesting experiment; I wish to see whether everything that befalls me will strengthen me; whether I will withstand or not."[13] But even in exile Pavlova, who was never closed to life, was able to form her last great literary friendship with a man who treated her not as a monster but as an admired equal,

Alexei Konstantinovich Tolstoi, the poet, playwright, and humorist. They met in Dresden in 1860 and she translated his poetry and plays into German so that they were acclaimed outside his native country. As his letters show, she also helped him with the Russian originals.[14] He in turn secured a pension for her from the Russian government and corresponded warmly and solicitously with her until his death in 1875. Pavlova outlived him by eighteen years and died worse than reviled, forgotten.

II

To be more than charitable we might say that Pavlova's life and art were so badly misread by her contemporaries because she was such a unique phenomenon in Russia. The eminent scholar B. Ya. Bukhshtab writes of how the first century of the new Russian poetry, from 1740-1840 approximately, brought forth not one notable woman author.[15] Pavlova's only contemporary female poet of note, the Countess Evdokiia Rostopchina, was as different from Pavlova herself as were the different cities in which they lived, St. Petersburg and Moscow. Rostopchina's poetry, aside from being stylistically less interesting than Pavlova's, reads more like a chronicle of her vastly more successful life. This more intimate, domestic sort of poetry ("I am only a woman . . . ready to be proud of this," Rostopchina wrote in her lyric "Temptation") was and is generally considered peculiarly appropriate to women writers. Pavlova's own verse, its feeling restrained, the lyric meditation or elegy her preferred genre, was considered by her contemporaries as it was by the modern Russian poet Khodasevich as "above all not feminine."[16] Pavlova's lyrics, for example the cycle of poems inspired by her love for Boris Utin, can hardly be termed cold and abstract, but even when her poems reflect personal emotion, the feeling is

xi

both intensified and generalized, as is true in the case of most good poetry.

Neither are Pavlova's longer poems or her prose works a kind of confessional: still Pavlova's treatment of the theme of woman is central to many of them. Here as well she was able to turn from the exact circumstances of her own life to the whole condition of the lives of others like her, the Russian women of her class. (Pavlova has no illusions about an aristocrat really being able to fathom the depths of misery of Russia's poor, and she mocks Cecily, the heroine of *A Double Life*, for thinking that poverty can somehow be graceful.)

Pavlova's works have never been discussed critically in terms of the primary theme that would link them to her life. Critics contemporary both with her and with us have pretended that her treatment of women is no more than a mere aspect of a criticism of aristocratic Russian society in general. But especially in a few of her longer poems and in her prose works, Pavlova concerned herself in a primary sense with women's "fate"—fate in quotation marks to stress the fact that if her women fail to be the agents of their destiny it is not because their nature dooms them to suffering, but because the actions of men determine their fate. She described especially keenly the peculiar amorphousness of women's lives, of what is expected and not expected of them, or, as she called it in her long narrative poem "Quadrille," "the confusion *(bestolkovost')* of woman's role—/ A mixture of willfulness and constraint/ Which is nearly always our lot." The willfulness of a young girl who is seemingly free to accept or reject any man she wants and to construct her own dreams of life, and the constraint that the narrowness of her upbringing, the rules of acceptable conduct in society, and the ultimate necessity of marriage impose on her form part of the duality of *A Double Life*.

In various of her other writings Pavlova described later stages of a woman's life as well, although she had no definite comprehensive plans to be complete in this respect. In "Quadrille," published in 1859 but begun as early as 1843, four women who are already married tell each other their stories, recalling how in different ways their girlish illusions have been shattered. In her memoirs, which survive only in the fragment which was published in 1877, Pavlova, in the midst of a description of her own happy childhood, gives us a portrait of the death of a very old lady, a creature from a previous age. Again we see the paradoxical quality of a woman's existence, bound by convention yet full of strange heroic independence. The old lady has nursed a breast cancer without telling anyone about it: "This pampered lady to whom the smallest inconvenience was a burden, suffered a tormenting pain over the years, without permitting herself a single outcry." She would lock herself in her bedroom and wash the blood and pus from her underwear so that even her maid wouldn't see it. Pavlova's father, who had a medical degree, was a close friend of the lady and suspected nothing. Pavlova expands the paradox:

> Seeing a doctor every day, in whose art she fully believed, she had the strength of spirit not to betray herself even once, not to ask for help or the alleviation of the disease which was killing her! And all from modesty, in order not to have to bare her breast before a doctor—her breast of a sixty-year-old woman! One can call that folly, but it is impossible not to recognize a heroism of sorts in a woman who, awaiting an inescapably near and agonizing death, to the very end did not allow herself the slightest slight to decorum, the most negligible digression from accustomed rules, did not once forget to embellish her clothes with the appropriate ribbon, to rouge her cheeks, and affix a mouche to her face.[17]

This strange behavior is the logical end of the upbringing to which young girls were subjected—and a true story stranger than any fiction. Russian realism had to pretend to a semblance of believability; Russian reality didn't.

While Pavlova felt a generalized sympathy with all the ages of woman, all "mute sisters of my soul" as she called them in her dedicatory poem to *A Double Life*, she still felt closest to people of keen intelligence and to poets. Most of her heroines are not she. Like Cecily in *A Double Life*, their talents are unconscious, suppressed by circumstances of their lives as Pavlova never allowed hers to be. A long story of 1859 called *At Tea* begins with a sharp debate about the lack of equality of the sexes and whether women's dependency and inferiority are inevitable. One character asserts that women are educated to be child-like and then politely scorned as having childish minds; the other says a woman's nature is different from a man's. Later on a story within the story is told and its main character, the Countess Aline, says to a man who wants to marry her:

> Don't you know that to praise a woman's intelligence means to reprove her? Aren't people all convinced that there is no heart? Hasn't it been decided that an intelligent woman is some kind of monster that has no feelings? Ask anyone; anyone will tell you this.[18]

Pavlova's own bitterness emerges at times untransmuted by the more generalized passion of her art.

While Pavlova was nearly alone among Russian women writers of her time in the realization of her ambition to be a poet of importance, she was also part of the beginning of a new kind of literary activity in Russia, one concerning women and often involving women writers. In the second third of the nineteenth century, while women were beginning to write in the popular journals of the day, critics eagerly debated whether women should or shouldn't write and what was woman's special sphere of talent as a writer. Related to this phenomenon was the fact that in the 1830s male writers were developing the possibility of the society tale for social criticism and psychological intrigue. Still earlier, in France, Madame de Genlis had perfected this genre. In her story "La Femme Auteur," she even confronts this problem of the woman writer: "Men would never accept a woman author as an equal, they would be more jealous of her than of a man."[19]

In Russia, Odoevsky refined this genre in the 1830s, and stories like his "Princess Mimi" (1834) or "Princess Zizi" (1839) have as their central figures independent, contradictory women who manipulate, if not their own destinies, then certainly those of others. If their lives produce evil results, then Odoevsky lets us know that their education is to blame: "They teach [a girl] dancing, drawing and music so that she may get married. . . . This is the beginning and end of her life. It *is* her life."

Lermontov sees the same social types, but much more from the man's point of view. In "Princess Ligovskaya" (1836), which formed the basis for part of *A Hero of Our Time*, the hero is one who is hurt by society, and women, whether unyielding ("the class of women who have no heart") or vulnerable, are damned either way. For women, says Lermontov, "tears are a weapon both for offense and for defense."

A third author of society tales, V. Sollogub, wrote at least one which probably had some influence on *A Double Life*, a story called *The Ball*. It describes how men and women both hide their feelings behind masks. In a dream, their real emotions surface, but only temporarily. The narrator is a man, but the woman he loves/hates has a long confessional monologue. Thus for a decade before Pavlova wrote *A Double Life* the prose writers of Russia were describing, with varying degrees of sympathy, women in society whose conflict with the world took place in the shrunken arena of their town houses, in their drawing rooms, behind their tea-tables. In these small places where they fought the determining battles of their lives, their strength is tested and their character defined as surely and dramatically as if they, like the men, had gone to the rugged mountains or limitless horizons of the Caucasus to pacify the natives and fight duels with fellow officers.

The publication of *A Double Life* in 1848, when Pavlova was at the height of her fame as a poet and translator, was a literary event which drew the attention of all the important literary journals of Russia. One chapter of the novel had been published a year before and the full work was eagerly anticipated. The fact that it was part prose and part poetry seemed to bother no one; the reviewers understood the purpose of this structure and praised the quality of the poetry highly. Even *The Contemporary*'s anonymous reviewer called Pavlova's new work "original in form, in the highest degree remarkable in content."[20] In one of the peculiar tributes women poets are subject to, he stated that the poetry was so sharp and energetic that "it is difficult to recognize in it the tender hand of woman." Showing his social conscience, he praised Pavlova for dealing with important questions like the education of society women. He also made the crucial distinction that the heroine carries poetry in her soul without actually being a poet. But his enthusiasm went far beyond the text and caused him to utter something contradictory to the ideas of the novel he had just been praising when he rhapsodized that young girls should certainly not try to lose their love of parties and cease to cultivate feminine charms:

> On the contrary, we would even wish our girls and especially women more of that desire to please. Maybe this would save them from the terrible change which comes over them when they get married, when they

xvi

no longer consider it necessary to dress nicely at home for their husbands, when they replace the corset with the peignoir, the slender figure with a full body....[21]

Here the male imagination indulging in literary and social criticism of a most fanciful kind, itself becomes *ex post facto*, a kind of background for what Pavlova was dealing with in her novel.

A Double Life, a novel in ten chapters, is the story of a young girl named Cecily von Lindenborn whom we see being trapped into a meaningless life and marriage by the people closest to her—her well-meaning mother, her best friend Olga, and Olga's mother, an experienced social manipulator. In the last chapter, Dmitry, Cecily's suitor, marries her for money. Pavlova does an excellent job of describing this kind of man of little will who is teased by his friends into a pledge of faithlessness to his marriage even before it takes place. As one of the bachelors says, "Who would want to get married if the blessed state of matrimony made it necessary to give up wine and good times?" Cecily, on the other hand, has only vague premonitions that something is going wrong. Her upbringing has so carefully cultivated an almost total ignorance that

she could never commit the slightest peccadillo . . . could never forget herself for a moment, raise her voice half a tone . . . enjoy a conversation with a man to the point where she might talk to him ten minutes longer than was proper, or look to the right when she was supposed to look to the left. . . .

Cecily, surrounded by wealth, friends, and family, is ultimately quite alone. Her mother—who accompanies Cecily almost constantly and communicates with her not at all, wants her married—to someone rich if possible, but married.

Her closest friend Olga encourages Cecily's marriage, so that she will be *hors de concours* for a certain disdainful Prince Victor, who goes off to Paris in the last chapter anyway, and in so doing foils the carefully laid plans of Olga's mother, Natalia Afanasevna. Clever as this prime mover of the intrigue underlying *A Double Life* may be, it is the men who always have the ultimate option of freedom.

Like most of the great Russian novels of its time, this one is set in the aristocratic world. Pavlova further logically restricts her heroine to the female quarters of this world—enclosed and protected in domestic interiors or carriages traveling from house to house or from house to church. In the rare moments when Cecily steps out onto a balcony or rides on horseback she experiences a short-lived sense of exhilaration and of control over fate: "She gave herself over to the joy of riding horseback, to the attractions of this living force, this half-free will that carried her off and that she was guiding." This is Pavlova's most potent sexual metaphor in the non-dream sections of the novel and probably the best that Cecily will be granted before or after her marriage.

Nevertheless, it is in the most secluded place, in her bedroom, that Cecily is the least constrained. Here we see the revelations of her mind freed from its mental corset (to use Pavlova's image). Every chapter has the same structure with variations—a day of society's vanities and cruelties followed by a night of dreams. Each chapter begins in prose and ends in verse, the verse a kind of interior monologue, to reflect the double life Cecily leads. The sections linking them are often in rhythmical prose and describe a state of drowsing, between reality and dream. There are other links as well: she dreams about people she hears about in the drawing room by day, and thinks in her waking hours of what she has seen in her dreams. Finally, dream and waking have an inverse emotional correlation: the better Cecily's real life seems to become as her marriage approaches, the greater the anguish expressed in her poetic dreams.

Each separate chapter has its own careful structure as well: the ninth, for example, begins and ends with Cecily's sad dreaming and contrasts in the middle the pre-wedding parties of bride and groom; the tenth begins in the brilliant but artificial illumination of Cecily's mother's house and ends with the church lights being extinguished after the wedding and a view of the dark empty street. And there is often a nice alternation of style from one chapter to the next: chapter six contains long descriptive or ironically didactic paragraphs; chapter seven deals with the machinations of Muscovite matrons predominantly in dialogue (as each says the opposite of what she thinks and the other knows it but must pretend to take her words at face value).

Within the well-planned framework of the novel are the equally important small touches—symbolic, ironic, humorous. Pavlova excells in the topography of social relations: who sits near whom, who walks with whom determines whole years of a character's life. The breaking of a blossom or closing of the latch on a jewelled bracelet symbolizes a future life broken and encircled. The most pathetic female character of all is named Nadezhda: she still has (what the name means) "hope" that she too will be married someday.

Pavlova, as unabashedly as any of the nineteenth century male writers, makes clear in her fiction her own preferences and values in life. Thus, its attitude towards poetry is the measure of the society of the novel. When a poet suffers and is ridiculed, society is condemned. Even Cecily dares set her creative mind free only in dreams; in her waking life she knew "that there were even women poets, but this was always presented to her as the most pitiable, abnormal thing, as a disastrous and dangerous illness." The behavior of the two sexes is unequally compared by Pavlova. She describes men posing as carefully as women in society (they are equal in vanity); but her men have a particular crudeness that her women are free of, and some of her women have certain attractive virtues which her men at best only seem to have—"that violent female daring which is so far from manly valor."

Pavlova possesses a romanticism characteristic of her time but mixed with an ironic sense of reality. We are told repeatedly that Cecily's love for Dmitry is good even though Dmitry himself is not. Cecily's mysterious sickliness both enhances her worldly beauty and brings her closer to the other world she dreams of. Cecily is vulnerable like two of the novel's minor characters—the poet who encounters boredom when he recites, and the dead wife who is reproached for having loved her husband too well. Nature and seasonal change play an important role, even in this society tale. The sounds of nature outside Cecily's room mark a transition from waking to dreams. Nature acts as an ironic accomplice to society when, in the gardens of a summer house, "even nature made itself unnatural." The starry expanse of sky often provides a contrast to the petty world below. The novel begins in spring when Cecily dreams of love and ends in autumn when she is married. The winter ahead is strongly implied.

The strength of this novel as of Pavlova's view of life is that both merge these romantic concepts into an ultimate clear realism. The countless ironic touches in *A Double Life*—from purely lexical ones such as the use of the word "satisfied" to larger metaphors like the one comparing marriage to a mother pushing her daughter out of the window onto the pavement below—prevent the reader from becoming too lost in the enjoyment of details of how rich aristocrats live. Similarly, as much as we could wish a happier ending for Cecily, Pavlova leaves her, and us, with the one weapon against life that does not destroy life—consciousness. The double awareness that this is the way things are and ought not to be, and the high quality of Pavlova's narrative and poetic style are themselves a vivid protest against the "destiny" of women.

NOTES

1. These and many other biographical facts have been discovered or confirmed by Munir Sendich. See his unpublished dissertation, "The Life and Works of Karolina Pavlova" (New York Univ., 1968), and his recent publications of Pavlova's correspondence: "Twelve Unpublished Letters to Alexey Tolstoi," *Russian Literature Triquarterly*, No. 9 (Spring 1974), pp. 541-58 and "Boris Utin in Pavlova's Poems and Correspondence: Pavlova's Unpublished Letters to Utin," *Russian Language Journal*, No. 100 (Spring 1974), pp. 63-88. The only other Pavlova scholar writing in English gives some singularly obtuse observations on her life and character but follows them with a useful analysis of her rhythmic innovations. See Anthony D. Briggs, "Twofold Life: A Mirror of Karolina Pavlova's Shortcomings and Achievement," *The Slavonic and East European Review* (January 1971), pp. 1-17.

2. N.M. Iazykov, *Polnoe sobranie stikhotvorenii* (M.-L., 1934), pp. 791-92.

3. B.N. Chicherin, *Vospominaniia. Moskva sorokovykh godov* (M., 1929), pp. 3-4.

4. A partial list would include Aleksandr Turgenev, Chaadaev, Herzen, Khomiakov, Konstantin and Ivan Aksakov, Granovski, Pogodin, Shevyrev, Fet and Polonski, and foreign visitors such as Franz Liszt and Alexander von Humboldt. See Munir Sendich, "Moscow Literary Salons: Thursdays at Karolina Pavlova's," *Die Welt der Slaven*, Jahrgang XVII, Heft 2 (1973), pp. 341-57.

5. I.N. Pavlov, "Iz moikh vospominanii," *Russkoe obozrenie*, No. 4 (1896), p. 889.

6. A.S. Khomiakov, *Polnoe sobranie sochinenii* (M., 1904), VII, 102. This is in a letter of Khomiakov's wife Ekaterina to Iazykov who was her brother.

7. N. Kovarskii, Introduction to Karolina Pavlova, *Polnoe sobranie sochinenii* (L., 1939), pp. vi-vii.

8. I.I. Panaev, *Literaturnye vospominaniia* (L., 1928), pp. 288-89.

9. D.V. Grigorovich, *Literaturnye vospominaniia* (L., 1928), p. 193.

10. A letter of 23 January 1860 in *I.S. Aksakov v ego pis'makh*, III (M., 1892), p. 353.

11. Quoted in Boris Rapgof, *K. Pavlova, Materialy dlia izucheniia zhizni i tvorchestva* (P., 1916), pp. 18-19.

12. Letter of 12 October 1854 quoted in Karolina Pavlova, *Sobranie sochinenii*, ed. V. Briusov (M., 1915), II, pp. 330-32.

13. Rapgof, p. 73. One critic in a recent biography of her husband claims that Pavlova led a life of luxury abroad (V.P. Vil'chinskii, *N.F. Pavlov* (L., 1970), p. 101). Quite the opposite is true. Nearly all her unpublished letters of the time admit to financial as well as moral distress. See, for example,

two letters in the Manuscript Division of the Saltykov-Shchedrin Library, Fond 852, N. 784 and Fond 66, N. 1, pp. 46-47. The latter reads: "Je suis hors d'état d'agir, incapable même de vouloir, et horriblement seule."

14. A.K. Tolstoi, *Sobranie sochinenii*, IV, pp. 329, 347 and *passim*.

15. See B. Ia. Bukhshtab, ed., *Poety 1840-1850kh godov* (M.-L., 1962), p. 35.

16. V. Khodasevich, "Odna iz zabytykh," *Novaia zhizn'*, III (1916), p. 198.

17. Pavlova, ed. Briusov, II, 303.

18. *Ibid.*, 383.

19. Madame de Genlis, *Nouveaux contes moraux et nouvelles historiques* (Paris, 1804), III, pp. 61-62.

20. Anon., "Dvoinaia zhizn'. Ocherk K. Pavlovoi," *Sovremennik*, VII, No. 3 (1848), p. 47.

21. *Ibid.*, pp. 52-53.

A DOUBLE LIFE

Our life is twofold: Sleep has
its own world,
A boundary between the things
misnamed Death and existence.

Byron

DEDICATION

To you the offering of this thought,
The greeting of my poetry,
To you this work of solitude,
Slaves of din and vanity.
In silence did my sad breath name
You Cecilys unmet by me,
All of you Psyches without wings,
Mute sisters of my soul!
May God grant you too, unknown family,
Just one bright dream mid sinful lies,
In the prison of this narrow life
Just one brief burst of that other life.

September 1846

I

"But are they rich?"

"I think so; the estate is sizable. They live well enough. Besides the usual Saturdays they give several balls during the winter; he himself doesn't enter into things; his wife handles everything; *c'est une femme de tête.*"

"What's the daughter like?"

"Nothing special! Good-looking enough and not stupid, they say, but who is stupid nowadays? Anyway I've never discussed anything with her except the weather and dances, but she must have a touch of her father's German blood. I can't stand all these Germans and half-Germans."

"A good match?"

"No! There's a younger brother."

"What do people do there on Saturdays?"

"Well, they mostly talk. Not too many people there. You'll see."

"Oh, I'm so fed up with conversations! You can't escape from them."

The carriage stopped at the entrance of a large house on Tverskoi Boulevard.

"Here we are," said one of the two young men who were sitting in it, and both got out and ran up the wrought iron staircase. In the vestibule they made sure with a glance that their German-tailored clothing was fitted just right, they entered, bowed to their hostess, and looked around.

In the elegant drawing room were about thirty people. Some were talking among themselves in low tones, some were listening, others passing through, but it seemed as if all of them were weighed down by a sense of duty, evidently quite onerous, and it seemed they all found amusing themselves a bit boring. There were no loud voices or arguments, nor any cigars either. This was a drawing room completely *comme il faut;* even the ladies did not smoke.

Not far from the door sat the hostess on one of those nondescript pieces of furniture that fills our rooms these days. In another corner stood a tea-table. Nearby some exceedingly nice young girls were whispering among themselves. A bit further away, next to a large bronze clock on which 10:30 had just struck, a very noteworthy gracious woman sunk, so to speak, in a huge velvet armchair, was conversing with three young men sitting near her. They were talking about someone.

"He died this morning," one of them said.

"Nothing to mourn about," answered his lovely neighbor with an extraordinarily nice glance at him.

"Well," said one youth, smiling, "he was not so young any more but very good-looking, he was wicked but clever."

"He was simply unbearable," said the lady, "and I never liked his looks; there was something angry about them."

"Who died?" softly asked a graceful, pale, dark-haired girl of eighteen, going up to the tea-table and bowing to one of the ladies near it. "Who died, Olga?"

"I don't know," Olga replied.

The dark-haired girl sat down at the table and started to pour tea.

The gracious lady in the velvet armchair continued her clever conversation with the three young men. Judging by the words of that conversation, it was limp and banal enough, but to judge by the expressions, the smiles and glances of the people talking, it was extremely lively and intricate.

"Who is that, Cécile?" Olga whispered to the young girl pouring tea.

Cecily looked up.

"The man who came in with Ilichev? I forget his name. It's the first time he's ever come to our house. It seems he's a poet."

Olga gave a haughty pout and turned her head toward the other side of the room. Two more men appeared. One of them led the other to the hostess, Vera Vladimirovna von Lindenborn, and introduced him. She greeted them most pleasantly.

"I am truly glad to be able to meet you at last. I hope that some time you will give us the pleasure of hearing you read your work."

Vera Vladimirovna was not only a highly-educated woman who entertained poets and artists, but also a woman of tact. She did not wish to put her visitor's talent to use the very first time.

In the opposite corner of the drawing room a distinguished man with graying hair barely perceptible in the candlelight, with a certain artificial carelessness in his dress and pretentions to profundity and perspicacity went up to a young dandy who, leaning towards the window, profiled to his satisfaction his eccentric hairstyle and his spotless gloves very successfully against the heavy cherry-colored curtain that fell to the parquet floors and set off his tie of the latest Parisian cut. He did not even contemplate having any other affectation.

"Look at the group near the tea-table," the distinguished man said to him, "Shall I tell you what is going on there? Sophia Strenetsky is wondering where she can find a magnanimous bridegroom who will rescue the family from inevitable poverty and clear their debts to the Trusteeship Council. Olga Valitsky is out of sorts because Prince Victor has not come. Princess Alina is smiling so

5

hard in vain; the victorious Uhlan is not going to leave her cousin today, and she is using him to bedevil a certain other gentleman. Isn't it amusing?"

"You're a terrible man!" the young dandy respectfully answered, twirling his whiskers.

The terrible man smiled condescendingly.

In the mature ladies' circle the conversation was more innocent.

"Will you be moving to your summer place soon?" Vera Vladimirovna was asked by a tall, important-looking lady sitting next to her, who until then had observed a strict silence.

"In about two weeks, at the beginning of June," she answered. "It seems the bad weather has passed. Will you be at yours too?"

"Yes, I love it. At least there you can spend the summer in good society, not like in the country where you meet with God knows what kind of neighbors."

"I agree completely," said another well-dressed lady of forty who wore roses in her hair and short sleeves as a kind of antidote against old age. "I am terribly glad to have escaped the district of Ryazan. My husband was absolutely set on taking me there for the summer, but thanks to my brother's wedding I'm lucky enough to end up in Petersburg instead of Ryazan. Even here in Moscow I'm feeling a little stifled."

"You're an enemy of Moscow," remarked Vera Vladimirovna.

"Why? I only share the opinion of Napoleon and think that, except for two or three drawing rooms such as this one, Moscow is a large village. And I admit I'm not devoted to villages."

Meanwhile the pouring of tea ceased, and Cecily and the young girls went out on the wide balcony. It was a magnificent May night, full of stars. The lindens grown green in front of the balcony rustled so softly, so sadly, so mysteriously, that it seemed as if they were growing not on the Tverskoi Boulevard but in the free expanse of virgin nature. Cecily leaned on the iron railing and became lost in thought about heaven knows what.

Her friends were laughing among themselves. One, a lively blonde girl, her back to the railing, looked through a lorgnette at the drawing room and made her remarks in a semi-whisper. She was obliged to make fun of people because she had the reputation of being very witty.

"I think," she said, "that blue dress has been worn for so long it will soon need something to hold it up."

The girls almost burst out laughing.

One of them asked, "Doesn't my brother's uniform become him?"

"Not at all," said the blonde girl. "A man in a uniform should be swarthy and dark-haired, like Chatsky for example. Don't you agree, Cecily, that Chatsky is very handsome?"

"Not in my opinion," Cecily answered. "His features are too sharp. I like a man to have a modest appearance and even an almost feminine shyness."

"Where is Dmitry Ivachinsky?" the blonde girl suddenly asked her.

"He's visiting his father in the country," said Cecily in a voice that showed she was blushing.

"When is he coming back?" the blonde continued with a meaningful smile.

"How should I know?" Cecily turned and went into the drawing room again.

Some mothers were already looking for their daughters, to take them home. Vera Vladimirovna came up to Cecily.

"Time to sleep, Cécile," she said. "You know that doctor's orders are for you to go to bed early, and it's already almost midnight. Go on, people will understand." She made the sign of the cross over her and Cecily went out, walked past a long series of rooms, lighted and dark, turned into a barely lit corridor and went into her own room.

There everything was peaceful and silent. In the adjoining room her old Englishwoman had already been in a deep sleep for two hours.

As is well known, a girl of the highest circles cannot be without an Englishwoman. In our society we do not speak English, our ladies generally read English novels in French translations, and Shakespeare and Byron are completely beyond their reach, but if your six-year-old daughter speaks otherwise than in English, she is badly educated. It often follows that the mother, not as well-educated as her daughter, has trouble talking to her, but this inconvenience is of slight importance. A child needs an English nurse more than a mother.

Cecily called to the maid and began to undress slowly and pensively. She was thinking that most likely the summer would be pleasant, that the summer house would be fun, that soon Dmitry Ivachinsky would return and that they would take walks together and dance and go horseback riding. But at the same time in the midst of these happy thoughts a strange and inexplicable one kept breaking through, a heavy and persistent feeling, as if she were being made to guess a riddle, find a word, remember a name and was not able to... Finally she lay down, the maid went out carrying the candle and everything grew quiet. In the cozy, soundless room the small lamp flickered in front of the ikon of the Savior.

The clock on the small column between the windows struck 12:30 with one loud stroke in the silence. Cecily's glance wandered lazily around the bedroom. At moments she could see the peaceful ikon in its dazzling frame; at moments it was invisible. Then drowsiness closed it from her sight... but the question in her soul did not sleep... what was it?... who?... and where?...

8

The heavenly vault shone with stars...
The mist was dispelled...a fragrance wafted in...
Is this a chamber, airy and wondrous?
Is this a rich and moonlit garden?
How clear is the sleepless lament of the fountain!
How familiar to her the bounds of the unknown!
Bowing to her with a fragrant caress,
All around the timid flowers shine.
The moon is silent in the depths of air,
Like a clear pearl in the sea's boundlessness;
An empty answer sounds in the leaves,
Like a whispering lyre, and is borne into the distance.
And the midnight radiance of all the worlds,
And all the sighs, gliding through silence,
And all the fragrant breaths of spring
Melt into a single harmony.

    What secret knowledge
    Troubles her young soul?
    Whom does she wait for,
    Whose arrival does she sense?
    Over whom have sycamores bowed down?
    What will shine bright in that darkness?—
    Commanding gaze,
    Victorious brow.
    She remembers what never was,
    Recognizes what she has never met.
    He is reflected in the mirror of her thoughts
    Like the light of a star in a mirror of water.
    He stands, powerful and stern,
    Stands unmoving and silent;
    He looks into her eyes with his eyes,
    Looks into her soul with his soul.
    What reproach of guilt, of error,
    Brings a frown to that brow?
    On that unsmiling countenance

What a melancholy love!
What lay so heavy on the young girl's heart
Like an inescapable sentence?...
She walks—walks against her will
Across distances ever more silent
To where, powerful and despondent
That glance shines, like a summons.
And she stood before the unknown force,
Bowing a submissive head.
And from his lips there came a word
Sadder than the song of far-off strings;
It seemed as if a quiet kiss
Had touched her youthful brow.

gloves. With the topographical knowledge of ladies they rode far and wide in Moscow—from Miasnitskaya Street to the Arbat, from the Arbat to the Petrovka—and finally to the study of Madame Valitsky, the mother of Cecily's best friend Olga Alexeevna.

Madame Valitsky, a very rich woman, a woman extremely stern in all her opinions and judgments, fully earned the respect of high society, for which neither the future nor the past exists. Zealously she paid her debt of virtue and morality, all the more so because she had gotten a bit of a late start. She had not thought much about such a debt for the better half of her life, but then, having been convinced of its necessity, she—one must do her justice—endeavored with incredible zeal to pay the aforementioned debt and all interest which had accrued.

Most likely there is no person so inexperienced as to be surprised that Vera Vladimirovna, in spite of her customary chastity and her implacable rules of conduct, was on friendly terms with Madame Valitsky. Who would think of worrying about the past youth of a woman who for ages had led the most decorous life and, moreover, who received the best society, gave magnificent balls and was always ready to do a favor for her friends? The stern world is sometimes very good-natured: according to circumstances it looks with such Christian forgiveness upon powerful people, upon prominent and wealthy women! And besides, in the aristocratic educated world everything is angled so smoothly, the sharp edges so blunted and each monstrous and rotten affair called by such decent language that every shameful thing is glossed over in such fine circumstances, effortlessly and quietly. If some ignoramus in some drawing room recalled Madame Valitsky's past adventures, he would not have found anyone who knew anything about them, and he would have been told it was a calumny invented about an intelligent and sweet woman who in her youth perhaps had been just a bit flighty. In general in society gatherings they don't like to speak about vice, probably for the same reason that in olden times they didn't like to refer to the devil, fearing his presence.

And so, Madame Valitsky in the midst of such civilized company was, as they say in that foreign language, *parfaitement bien posée*. Vera Vladimirovna found particular profit in this friendship. The tone of Madame Valitsky's drawing room satisfied her wishes fully. She knew that nowhere would she find a more strict and careful circle of friends, that nowhere would Cecily be safer, that here she would not hear a single light-minded word or remark. And experience showed to what extent Vera Vladimirovna was right, because—as the French proverb goes, in the house of a hanged man they don't talk about rope—so at Natalia Afanasevna Valitsky's they didn't even talk about thread.

When she found out about Cecily's arrival, Olga Valitsky went hurriedly into her mother's room. The young girls, although they had parted only the evening before, embraced as if they had been separated for a year, sat on the sofa in the corner, whispered together for a few minutes, and then jumped up again.

"Maman," said Olga, "we're going to my room." She slipped through the door with Cecily.

Vera Vladimirovna looked after them:

"How pretty Olga has become!" she remarked.

"Cécile is twice as pretty," answered Madame Valitsky, "but you have to look after her health more carefully; she is still a bit downcast. You are right not to take her to Anna Sergeevna's ball today."

"Yes, it's wiser. I won't go either although yesterday the Princess begged me to. What a lovely and praiseworthy woman!"

"A good mother is a rare thing," said Madame Valitsky.

"Or a happy mother," added Vera Vladimirovna, "Prince Victor is a remarkable young man."

13

Madame Valitsky's face assumed an important expression and she looked down modestly, saying, "Unfortunately, one cannot fully approve his conduct."

"Of course," answered Vera Vladimirovna in a voice resonant with Madame Valitsky's moral intonation, "but we must not judge him too harshly. Where can one find a young man who would not more or less deserve the same reproach? And then, time erases everything, and a virtuous wife can completely reform a flighty husband."

Madame Valitsky cast a momentary glance at her friend that meant "Aha," and barely perceptibly bit her lips.

"I thought of not going to that ball myself," she said, "but Olga begged me to. She very much wants to see the young people it's being given for. What a child she is! She dances and amuses herself like a ten-year-old. I don't mind in the least. You know I completely share your views on upbringing and have to admit that you couldn't apply them with more success. Cécile is the best proof of their correctness."

Vera Vladimirovna began to play with her lorgnette with self-satisfied modesty.

"Yes, I have to admit that my efforts have not failed. Cécile is exactly what I wanted to make of her. Every kind of daydreaming is foreign to her. I knew how to make reason important to her and she will never occupy herself with empty infatuations; but naturally I haven't, so to speak, taken my eyes off her."

"The first obligation of a mother," remarked Madame Valitsky. "We should aways be able to read into the souls of our daughters, in order to foresee any harmful influences and keep them safe in all their childlike innocence."

While the mothers were conversing thus in the study, their daughters were carrying on a completely different kind of conversation in Olga's room. The elderly Englishwoman was also there, but all her attention was turned to

14

some endless quilt she had been working on from times immemorial. Besides, like all our Englishwomen she scarely understood more than twenty Russian words and so Olga, sitting next to her friend, immediately began speaking Russian.

"So you won't be taken to the Princess' ball tonight?"

"No, maman says that I'm too tired and have to take care of myself."

"Well, you do look quite pale today; what's the matter?"

"My head aches; I slept badly. Imagine, Olga, I had a dream about the man they were talking about yesterday at our house, the one who had died that morning."

"God protect you! Who is it?"

"I don't know myself; remember at the tea-table they were talking about someone?"

"You are always having dreams about nonsense and various horrible things. What a shame that you're not going to the ball! It's being given for the young people, and they say it will be wonderful. The daughter's gown comes from Paris. Do you want to see my dress?"

Without waiting for an answer, Olga rang the bell.

"Masha! Bring out my dress."

The maid carried in a lovely, airy dress with a waist decorated with marvelous ribbons, a double skirt, one falling on top of the other like a rosy mist, an exquisite dress! Cecily looked at it and fully appreciated its worth.

"Who made it? Madame André?"

"Yes, she agreed to against her will; eleven dresses have been ordered from her for tonight. I was scared to death she wouldn't do it. How disappointing you aren't going! I am engaged for nearly every dance; I've promised the mazurka to Prince Victor."

"Is Prince Victor going to Petersburg?" asked Cecily in a semi-whisper.

Olga lowered her eyes and replied even more quietly:

"I don't know; maybe he'll go."

"You mean if you wish it?"

"No, darling," Olga whispered, clasping her friend's hand, "not yet. God knows what will happen. Only, for God's sake, don't tell anyone. Maman has strictly forbidden me to say a word about it, especially to you. You know she thinks you want to marry Prince Victor yourself. She doesn't know you're thinking about someone else."

Cecily smiled and in a few minutes the maid Masha announced: "Cecily Alexandrovna! Your mother has sent for you; she wants to leave right away."

Both friends ran downstairs. Vera Vladimirovna was already standing with Madame Valitsky in the hall ready to set out for home. The old friends shook hands, the young ones embraced three times and finally parted.

On the staircase of her house Vera Vladimirovna met her nephew.

"Hello, Serge! Where are you going?"

"I dropped in to ask how you are, ma tante, and now I'm off to Ilichev's. I'm having dinner with him at Chevalier's."

"Well, I don't want to keep you. Goodbye, my friend."

She went up several steps and stopped again. "A propos, Serge, listen!"

"What is it, ma tante?"

"You probably know that young man. What's his name? The one Ilichev introduced me to yesterday, the writer."

"Yes, I know, ma tante."

"Do me a favor, bring him to me next Saturday so that he can read us something. Yesterday evening was not a success for some reason, and next Saturday will be the last one, so I have to fill it up with something or other. It's a real penance!"

"All right, ma tante, I'll get the writer for you."

16

"Please don't forget."

"For heaven's sake!"

The nephew ran downstairs; the aunt went to her room.

Nearly all Vera Vladimirovna's acquaintances were at the ball that day, so she spent a very quiet evening at home. Still, two old ladies and one no longer young dropped in. They and their hostess made a foursome for a game of preference, the best way to pass the time in such circumstances. Vera Vladimirovna's husband (he was generally referred to as the husband of Vera Vladimirovna, and once when a stranger asked him with whom he had the pleasure of speaking he introduced himself thus) — Vera Vladimirovna's husband was, as always, at his club.

Cecily had a bad headache toward evening. After pouring the tea she asked permission to go to bed.

"Of course, my dear," said her mother, "but shouldn't we send for the doctor?"

"No, maman, it's nothing. By tomorrow I'll be fine."

She kissed her mother's hand, went to her room and lay down.

An unusual weariness, probably the result of her morning visits, took hold of her. She didn't know why, but her heart felt heavy. She lay down for a long time without sleeping, her eyes closed. Tiredness weighed her down more and more. Her thoughts grew still; a dream flew in to her. She forgot everything, but through that forgetfulness, some indistinct memory melted and grew clear in the depths of her soul. It seemed as if someone spread a misty veil over her head and she let herself down softly, softly, softly — suddenly a shiver ran through her body:

As if a miracle had been accomplished...

"As you were yesterday, you're here with me again!"

"I'm here with you, and will be faithful to you!

I've waited for you, I whom you called for, yours."

17

"Who are you?"
                    "The one you sought
In the radiance of starry heights.
I am your sadness in the tumult of a ball,
I am the secret of your dream
That you could not reach with reason,
That you have understood with your heart.
Have you not gone beyond the boundaries
Of the rich world to which you brought your
                                    thoughts?
Weren't you filled with the unknown,
Didn't you look into the distance?
Not knowing loss, still
Didn't you miss something all the same?"

They sit in the moonlight,
And a silver stream sings to them.
"Yes, it's you! You have come from the grave, alive!
Is it possible, or am I dreaming?"

"How may a creature of the earth know
What is impossible or possible?
Perhaps everything there was false,
Perhaps only here you are awake.

That prisoner of society's world,
That sacrifice to vanity,
The blind slave of custom,
That small-souled being isn't you.

They have forged you from childhood
Have swaddled your free mind,
Deprived it of its heritage,
Freedom of feeling and the kingdom of thought.

18

And under the iron yoke of the age
Joyful impulses were silenced in your heart,
But in the sinful human body
God's spirit has remained alive.

So only for a fleeting moment
You take wing with a free soul.
In life's deadness there is an incorporeal region
In the midst of that world another world.

You will understand inspiration's secret,
You will live the soul's life fully.
What the genius learns in waking
You will learn, my child, in sleep.

Yet you will forget what you have learned.
I will not poison your days,
I will not lift the veil
From your eyes, in that land of the blind.

And there my word will fall silent
The traces of my love will disappear;
Mid people's talk you will remember
Me like an empty dream.

But the spirit of silence will enter,
The world will fall asleep like a quiet house,
And, flaming with prayer,
The stars will stand before their creator.

And I will come to you unknown,
In the quiet, in a marvelous dream;
With the mysterious force of a kiss
I will lift the shackles from your soul,

So that the holy song may sound,
And holy incense rise,
And the divine service flame up
Again in you, the silent temple.

III

Vera Vladimirovna's final Saturday was a huge success: the coveted poet appeared. The company that evening consisted of the most select lovers of literature, both men and women. These days it is not at all difficult to get such a group together since literature is extremely respected, and ladies especially have been getting so involved in it for some time that only by hardly noticeable signs is it possible to guess that in fact they play no living role in it.

And so the poet appeared, a shy, rather awkward young man, his gloves not quite fresh. He entered with some feelings of timid pride into the well-lighted and enlightened drawing room where so many important persons, so many beautiful women had gathered to hear him. But right now they all had something else on their minds: Vera Vladimirovna's nephew had unexpectedly brought her a traveller just arrived in Moscow, a Spanish count, terribly interesting, a swarthy proud Carlist with sparkling eyes. Naturally he became the object of general attention, the focus of all female glances and the focus of the drawing room. All the ladies present were busy trying with fervent effort to please the new arrival, to ingratiate themselves with the foreign visitor by that well-known, incurable hospitality which is sometimes so fond and jealous that it becomes a bit indecent, and often makes us appear comical and our foreign guests arrogant. The poor man of letters stood in a corner, completely unnoticed. But what is so surprising in the fact that no one so much as glanced at him in such an unforeseen event? For Moscow ladies, men of letters are nothing unusual, but a Spanish count is still something of a novelty.

But after a couple of hours the count left, and then the hostess turned her attention to the poet. She went up to him and told him in a very nice way of her own and everyone else's impatience for and expectation of the recital he had promised. Then she seated him by a table with the audience around him, herself magnanimously occupying the most prominent place nearest him, where it would be impossible either to whisper or to yawn. The poor young man was a bit troubled and began to turn the pages of his notebook, not knowing what to select from it. Everything he did made it clear that it was the first time that he was preparing to deal with this class of people, who are separated from the rest of humanity and compose that proud "world of fashion" as it is so naively called, for which no other world exists in the Lord's universe.

Since Cecily and other young ladies were there, the recital had to be completely moral and blameless, and the timid poet after some hesitation finally decided to read his unpublished translation of Schiller's "Bell." He coughed and said in a modest voice, "The Song of the Bell." A minute's silence followed, a few graceful heads leaned forward, some rosy lips smiled sweetly, some lovely listeners fixed affable looks upon the young poet, while making a mental note that this was a very long piece. Emboldened by such flattering attention, the young man began to read, at first in a soft voice, then in a louder and livelier one. He was so young and inexperienced that he read his verse before that aristocratic society with the same passion with which he spoke them alone to himself in his modest room. He was so tempered in the flame of poetry that he did not sense

22

the worldly coldness of all these people. He placed before them a series of magically changing views: a peaceful childhood, a stormy youth and the ecstasy of love, and quiet happiness, and grief come from heaven, the flame of fire, the gloom of devastation and a mother's death, and then, in the distance, meadows in the light of evening with the herds slowly returning, the night quietly falling, healing calm and sudden terrible restlessness, joys of life and sorrows, ringing forth in the prayerful fateful sound of the bell, and finally from his burning lips the last inspired words flew:

> And henceforth may this be
> Its destiny
> Amid the heavens' expanse
> Carried high above earth,
> May it float, near to thunder
> And approach the world of stars.
> May its holy voice be higher
> Than all the constellation's choir
> May it praise the universe-creator
> And live a full life.
> With bronze tongue, it speaks
> Only of holy, powerful things;
> May time with her wings beat out of it
> All that is transient, hourly.
> And may it be the word of fate,
> Standing unconsciously above all,
> May it herald from afar
> The game of earth's reality,
> And startling us from on high
> With powerful sounds,
> May it teach us that all is not eternal,
> That all things earthly must pass.

The notebook fell from his hands. He fell silent.

"C'est délicieux! C'est charmant!" whispered a few voices.

Vera Vladimirovna repeated, with emotion, "C'est charmant!" and thanked the poet for the pleasure he had given them.

"How fine that was," said Cecily into Olga's ear.

"Very good," Olga replied, looking intently at someone through her lorgnette.

A short silence ensued.

"Yes," said a short, sweetly-smiling little man of about fifty, "that thought about time is a very felicitous one, but a bit drawn out in the German manner. With what strength and compression Jean-Baptiste Rousseau managed to express it in two lines:

> Le temps, cette image mobile
> De l'immobile Eternité."

One lady among the charming neighbors of the man of letters leaned close to him and asked sympathetically, "How long did this marvellous translation take you?"

"I don't know," answered the poor confused young man.

She turned away with a barely perceptible smile.

"That is really good poetry," said a lean serious man, Prince Somebody, quietly sitting in a large armchair, "but it's..." (he stopped for a moment, took a pinch of snuff, stretched his right leg over his left and continued) "but it's not very contemporary poetry. We are not content any more with empty dreaming; we demand action. In our century a poet should labor alongside this hard-working generation; poetry should be useful, it should hold vice up to shame or put a crown on virtue."

Vera Vladimirovna stood up for Schiller.

"Permit me, Prince," she remarked, "it seems to me that you are not quite right about the poem; there is much

24

that is morally edifying and truly useful in it."

"Yes," interrupted the Prince, inflamed by his own eloquence, "but it is all somehow not alive enough, not expressive enough. We want to see the point of a poem clearly. Understand this," he continued, turning to the poet, "your noble calling is more important now than ever, morally higher. Write poetry against coldhearted egotists, against the debauches of flighty young people, stir the conscience of the evil-doer, and then you will be a contemporary poet. We recognize only what is useful to mankind."

The poor young poet thought for a moment, perhaps, that to feel and to reason, to love and to pray—this too might be somewhat useful for humanity; but he was silent.

Vera Vladimirovna wanted to ask him to read another poem, but looking around, she saw that everyone seemed a bit wearied by the delights of poetry. Besides, it was already pretty late and her evening could end satisfactorily without the aid of any new artistic admixture. And indeed, this society of literary dilettantes gradually dispersed looking quite content, and their praises were even heard on the stairway:

"A young man with talent."

"And the Spaniard will be at my house tomorrow."

"He's very interesting."

"Marvellous eyes."

"What a pleasant evening!"

"Especially since it's over," a haughty youth added in passing, setting his hat to perch smartly on his brow.

An hour after the reading the rich drawing room was empty, and Cecily was sitting at her dressing-table, putting her heavy black hair up in curls for the night.

She felt somehow strange and awkward. Involuntarily she remembered and repeated some of the lines she had heard. Sharply delineated visions flashed by her again, and

25

all of this went quite beyond the customary bounds of her thoughts.

Cecily had been educated in the fear of God and society; the Lord's commandments and the laws of propriety carried equal weight with her. To destroy either even in thought seemed to her equally impossible and inconceivable. And although, as we have seen, Vera Vladimirovna greatly respected and loved poetry, she still considered it improper for a young girl to spend too much of her time on it. She quite justly feared any development of imagination and inspiration, those eternal enemies of propriety. She molded the spiritual gifts of her daughter so carefully that Cecily, instead of dreaming of the Marquis Poza, of Egmont, of Lara and the like, could only dream of a splendid ball, a new gown, and the outdoor fête on the first of May.

Vera Vladimirovna was, as we have seen, very proud of her daughter's successful upbringing, especially perhaps because it had been accomplished not without difficulty, since it took time and skill to destroy in her soul its innate thirst for delight and enthusiasm. Be that as it may, Cecily, prepared for high society, having memorized all its requirements and statutes, could never commit the slightest peccadillo, the most barely noticeable fault against them, could never forget herself for a moment, raise her voice half a tone, jump from a chair, enjoy a conversation with a man to the point where she might talk to him ten minutes longer than was proper or look to the right when she was supposed to look to the left. Now, at eighteen, she was so used to wearing her mind in a corset that she felt it no more than the silk undergarment that she took off only at night. She had talents, of course, but measured ones, decorous ones, *les talents de société,* as the language of society so aptly calls them. She sang very nicely and sketched very nicely as well. Poetry, as we have said earlier, was known to her mostly by hearsay as something wild and incompatible with a respectable life. She knew that there were even women poets, but this was always presented to her as the most pitiable, abnormal thing, as a disastrous and dangerous illness.

But now she was thinking involuntarily about that strange ability of the soul. Unconsciously there awakened in her a new and obscure sympathy for that harmony of verse, for those melodious thoughts, those improper delights, and this unexpected sympathy almost frightened her. Her reason told her that after all this was empty and unnecessary nonsense that shouldn't occupy her for long. And thinking this, she laid her graceful head on the pillow and was alone in the silence of the night. But no, through her drowsiness, poetry sounded in her again; she heard poetry and, half asleep, she smiled at the absurdity of this. But a persistent song hummed and sounded and lulled her. She heard it more clearly all the time, and its harmonies and inspired words appeared more and more real to her. It seemed as if waves were lifting her...she was in a small boat...carrying her far away...and then she glimpsed the shore; the moon came up...

The river flows and whispering goes
    The river's stream.
A boat is carried past, untiring
    Down the river.

A melody slips through the silence
    To meet a maiden
Like a far-off echo, like a musical
    Chord of waves.

And powerful, along with the wave
    Thoughts sing in her;
With a mighty sound there soars at night
    The flight of dreams,

Of dreams despondent and tense
Everything the mind has saved in vain.
Of the sad and shameless loss
Of greatest happiness and strength.
Of false worldly barriers,
Of intrigues of worldly judges
Of all those murdered without mercy
All who have died without a trace.

The river flows, and whispering goes
    The river's stream.
And with the maiden, untiring,
    The boat slips past.

It floats far at the current's will
    And the choir of stars
Far-shining, with a reproachful beam,
    Meets her glance.

The Milky Way leads to an endless world
    Far above her
And a heartfelt sigh flies sadly up
    To that eternity.

    "Perhaps with the passing years
    A better age will come:
    Mankind will not always be
    A sacrifice to worldly sin!
    Maybe days of hope
    Of blessedness are near,
    And holy yearnings once again
    Will start up in the soul.
    But why meet these reproaches
    Why perish vainly in the shadows,
    Prophets without usefulness,
    Whom God sends to earth today?

You drink to the dregs in vain
The bitter cup of life;
Your faith is alien to men,
They do not need your song."

And past, past untiring
The boat slips through;
The river flows and loudly goes
The river's stream.

And all the waves sing, pouring forth
A sonorous voice;
And the other distance, a mute region
Answers back.

The wind flying in the drowsing shade
Through the water's foam,
Through the roar, carries forth
A mighty answer.

And on they go amid upheavels
Hurling their loud verses at the world;
To them song is more than human striving,
Dreams are more necessary than worldly gifts.
Their conviction has no answer
Their inspiration no reward.
But, inaccessible to worldly power,
They sing. They do not create
For the empty joys of the masses—
For whom in vain life fills with miracles
The myriads of stars shine forth,
And the sun gleams in the heavens—
But so that people, sensing this mystery,
Will not be able to reject it;
So that the poet's alleluia
Will rise above earth's murmur:

29

Because for the universe this is
An inexhaustible blessing,
For holy gifts are everywhere
Where there is someone to understand them.
For every creature of the world
Must, fulfilling its existence,
Carry its own aura,
Shine with its own light through the darkness.
Not in vain in the distant desert
The sun for years had scorched the palm.
One day, tortured and burning,
Beneath it a lone head bowed down.
In the land of sterile heat
One man came near, his strength all gone.
He found nearby an hour of peace
And blessed the palm-tree's shade.

IV

Several days had passed since Vera Vladimirovna had moved into one of those nice pseudo-Gothic-Chinese buildings that Petrovsky Park is strewn with. Here too everything corresponded to the demands and conditions of society. Surrounding the luxurious cottage was a luxurious garden, its greenery always an excellent, a choice, one might say an aristocratic greenery. Nowhere a faded leaf, a dry twig, a superfluous blade of grass; banished was everything in God's creation that is coarse, vulgar, plebian. The very shrubbery around the house flaunted a kind of Parisian haughtiness, the very flowers planted in every available space took on a certain semblance of good form, nature made herself unnatural. In a word, everything was as it should be.

In the midst of this beautiful and artful decor, on a warm clear June evening, some saddled horses were standing. Three of them had ladies' saddles on them and fancy grooms alongside. Around them paced and fretted five or six young dandies, among them both Prince Victor and Dmitry Ivachinsky, who had only recently arrived. A little further away a large carriage and two light carriages for men were waiting, harnessed and ready. The ladies were sitting in the drawing room waiting for those who were riding and who were still getting into their riding habits. They finally appeared and the entire party went out onto the wide porch. Cecily and Olga, more slender than usual in long riding dresses of a dark color, even more graceful in black caps almost like those the men wore, under which

31

their thick hair tumbled out and their lively eyes shone, stopped on the iron steps, whips in hand, brave and beautiful. The restless horses were brought up to them. No sooner had they placed their narrow feet in the stirrups than off they flew. They flicked the reins and were carried far ahead of the men, with that violent female daring which is so far from manly valor.

The third horsewoman was one of those precious and useful friends with whom clever society women usually provide themselves. She belonged to the countless majority of ladies who have no money, no beauty and not even attractive minds—futile and insufficient substitutes for these two more important possessions. On the other hand, Nadezhda Ivanovna was essential to Madame Valitsky; Nadezhda Ivanovna shared in all the merriment of that brilliant circle and, poor thing, every day, without tiring, she set her thick figure, her thirty-year-old, ordinary face, her miserable dress alongside Olga's graceful figure, fresh face and marvellously artful clothes, and she probably did not understand herself how selfless she was being. Or maybe she did understand, how can we know? There are people who are ready to pay with the blood from their own veins in order to brush up against high society and as it were play a part in its amusements.

The destination of the ride was Ostankino.

The cavalcade, accompanied by the carriages, was already passing a cool, wide grove which the common folk, with their native good sense, chose for their amusements and made unquestionably their own, leaving the dusty Petrovsky Park and sandy Sokolniki to the more enlightened people. Cecily galloped forward. With childish joy she gave herself over to the fun of riding horseback, to the attraction of this living force, this half-free will that carried her off and that she was guiding. Besides, the late afternoon was beautiful, the meadows wide, the air invigorating, the sky endlessly clear. She struck her horse with the whip and went forward at top speed. A sort of incomprehensible intoxication possessed her. She suddenly wanted to gallop away from life's imprisonment, from all dependencies, from all obligations, all necessities. She rode with shining eyes, her hair flying loose. Suddenly someone caught up with her and someone's hand grabbed the reins of her horse and stopped it.

"Did the horse run away with you?" said Prince Victor.

Cecily came to her senses and caught her breath.

"No, I gave her free rein."

"How you frightened us," he continued, adding in a low voice, "How you frightened me!"

"I did?"

"You don't believe it?"

She smiled, straightened her hair, set her cap on her forehead and went on at a walk. The Prince stayed beside her and continued the conversation.

A few minutes later they heard a furious galloping, and Olga flew past them with Dmitry Ivachinsky. Olga was laughing.

But in the carriage Madame Valitsky didn't let her lorgnette fall from her eyes for a moment and was very preoccupied with Cecily. Vera Vladimirovna was sitting next to her with a face more contented than frightened and assured her friend that Cecily was an excellent rider and that her horse was very trustworthy and would never run away with her. Madame Valitsky could not convince herself of this and was so shaken that once or twice she had recourse to smelling salts.

Finally everyone arrived safely and galloped to the entrance of the Ostankino gardens. The men jumped down and helped the women, flushed with their exertion, from their mounts. In one of the pavilions tea, fruit and ice cream were being prepared for everyone. Meanwhile they set off for a walk. Cecily and Olga went on ahead, surrounded by the men. The cautious Vera Vladimirovna made sure at a glance that her obliging nephew Serge had fully understood a few words which she had whispered to him, that he was paying great attention to Olga, and that Prince Victor was next to Cecily. And the good mother, foreseeing all, accompanied by Nadezhda Ivanovna, followed behind the young people, very content with her strategic positionings. Madame Valitsky went last, having taken the arm of Dmitry Ivachinsky. She walked quietly and slowly, conversing with him about the charm of the evening and the cool freshness of Ostankino Park. Imperceptibly they lagged behind the others a little. Madame Valitsky continued the conversation in her mild quiet voice. (She always spoke in low tones.)

"It seems we are walking around the entire park. I'm afraid that the walk will last too long and that we will have to ride home in the twilight. What time is it now, Dmitry Andreevich? I haven't a watch."

Dmitry, who hadn't the least suspicion where that most innocent of questions, "What time is it?" can lead, took out his watch and answered simple-heartedly, "Quarter to eight."

"I don't know," continued Natalia Afanasievna, "whether I will permit Olga to go home on horseback. I'm always afraid of that ride. I just had a terrible fright seeing how Cecily's horse ran away with her."

"But Cecily Alexandrovna insists that the horse did not run away with her."

"Nonsense. I saw it myself. How is it that you didn't gallop after her immediately? She was a hair's breadth from death."

"Well, I...I didn't notice anything. She was ahead of me."

"That's just fine! But Prince Victor noticed right away and raced headlong to stop the horse."

Dmitry smiled faintly.

"That proves that Prince Victor is quicker than I."

Madame Valitsky smiled a little too, replying, "That may prove something else."

A smile remained on Dmitry's face.

"I think," he said, "that Prince Victor will never be subject to the danger of falling in love."

"Why? Cecily is extremely nice. And she will be a very good match. An old aunt decided to make Cecily her only heir after the death of her son. I know that for sure. The old lady has a considerable estate, and she isn't likely to live very long. Vera Vladimirovna was telling me only yesterday about this aunt's quite ill health. Vera Vladimirovna loves her sincerely and worries and grieves about her a great deal. Poor Vera Vladimirovna! An incomparably greater misfortune threatens her. Her young son is developing the same terrible disease which, as you know, killed three children of this unhappy mother in the first years of their lives. Cecily will probably remain her only consolation."

And with this sad thought, Madame Valitsky bowed her head and sighed, cutting short the conversation.

Dmitry Ivachinsky was a good man, even a noble man in the ordinary sense of the word, but why should a good and noble man not wish to be a rich man as well? As with the greater part of our generation, money, and even a lot of money, was the most essential element of life for him. He himself had a fine fortune, but what does a fine fortune serve for in our age if it only incessantly limits one's desires and makes one feel the need for wealth even more keenly and morbidly. He had liked Cecily for a long time, but he assumed her to be dowerless, so to speak, and calculated very sensibly and correctly that if he could only scrape by (as he expressed it) on fifteen thousand a year as a bachelor, then as a married man things would be bad for him. Besides, he was of limited intelligence; he looked only at what was pointed out to him, and now, following these indications, he saw Cecily for the first time in a different

35

light, one extraordinarily favorable to her. Decidedly he did not wish for the death of her brother or even of the old aunt, but since it was totally beyond his power to save the poor boy or the good old lady, he began to consider them already in their graves. And Cecily was decidedly a very sweet, very good-looking, and very good-hearted girl who could make a husband very happy.

Thinking about all this, Dmitry walked silently alongside Madame Valitsky, who was also silent, thinking how incredibly easy it is to manage things with certain people.

They returned to the pavilion where the servants were waiting with tea, and settled themselves. Madame Valitsky went up to her daughter who was standing some distance away, seemingly in order to fix her hair, which was completely dishevelled from the ride. This motherly work lasted about ten minutes, after which Olga took Cecily by the arm and went for a stroll with her around the expanse of the gardens. None of the men dared break into this friendly conversation. It was obvious that they were both speaking in a lively fashion, especially Olga. Her mother looked on from afar and was able to see that at first Cecily looked quite serious, but that soon she grew gayer and lowered her eyes with a very nice smile. Then Natalia Afanasievna turned to the table and with great pleasure began to eat the ice cream that had been put before her some time back.

When they had eaten and walked enough, they prepared to go home. Dmitry Ivachinsky led Cecily's horse up to her and put his hand down as a step for her graceful foot to mount.

"Cecily Alexandrovna," he said in a half-whisper, straightening her long dress, "let me ride beside you. The last time you frightened me so that I completely lost control."

"You had time to come to your senses," she replied.

"Oh. When I came to my senses, you had already

been saved by the chivalrous Prince, and I didn't dare bother you while you were thanking him."

Cecily, starting to laugh, slightly and very gaily, glanced quickly at Dmitry and galloped away. In that half-laugh, in that half-glance was the permission he asked for, and together they went through a green meadow, on which the twilight had already cast its shadow and the rising moon its pale light. The abandoned Prince Victor began to pay his attentions to Olga, considering this, in all the naiveté of his self-veneration, a cruel revenge for the insult Cecily had dealt him. The horses ran faster on the road home and soon reached their destination.

At the porch Dmitry jumped down and went to Cecily to help her dismount. She leaned forward and jumped, supporting herself on his uplifted hand, and in half a minute that protecting, firm hand clasped her soft little one as if it never wanted to let go. Cecily came hurriedly into the house, her face flushed, but no longer just from the ride.

And you, Vera Vladimirovna, in the fateful moment you were calmly getting out of the carriage. Where was your sharp eye, watchful mother? Where was your inevitable lorgnette?

It was already midnight when Cecily, having undressed, sent away the maid, and in a light peignoir sat down by the open window of her cozy room. The warm, almost still night air blew in on her face. Small clouds swept softly across the sky. There was emptiness all around. The magnificent night even took the haughty vulgarity from Petrovsky Park. Only the mysterious expanse of space was visible, only a mass of trees shone black, only the small light of peaceful dwellings glimmered somewhere. The broad-leafed maple in front of her window was rustling softly. In the distance the guard was walking back and forth singing. The slow Russian song sounded forth in the quiet, a song full of subdued sadness,

37

expansive, limitless, like its country.

For a long time Cecily sat in quiet, indefinite meditation. Finally, tired, she lay down, still listening to the despondent melody and hearing only her own thoughts and broodings. Sadly the far-off sounds put her to sleep; joyfully the dreams of her heart lulled her. The leaves under her window were whispering over and over...

> The Tsar orders everyone to serve;
> It happened long ago to my dear one.
> Everyone has been given a steed by the Tsar;
> No steed was given to my dear one,
> No steed was given for him to ride.
> My dear friend, use me as a hostage,
> Use me as a hostage, and then buy a horse.
> Serve for a while, you will finish that work;
> You will train the steed. You will rescue me.
> And they all came riding home,
> But no news of my dear one.
> The steed runs alone, and on it lies a token,
> On it lies a token, a feathered cap,
> My silken shawl is in this cap.
> I don't miss my shawl, carried in the cap,
> I miss my friend, now with another girl,
> With another girl; he quarrelled with me.

> A quiet hour, foggy spaces
> Warmth and emptiness;
> A strange rustling in the grove,
> The leaves whisper like mouths.
> The vale is dark and fragrant;
> Stars shine brightly in the sky.

> And the fountain, sparkling in the distance
> Scatters tears without number;
> It seems as if a quiet reproach

Were heard in the land.
In the heart young happiness
Has lain down with heavy grief.

There, like spirits of the night
Shadows go in black procession.
There, stern and powerful,
The fateful visitor arises.
Eyes were staring deeply
In the deep and silent gloom.

And flowing with the innate
Secret complaint of the quiet,
With the sadly whispering stream,
With the murmur of forest depths—
Surfeited with longing,
The soul's words poured forth:

"Be at peace! Be at peace! Why seek in vain?
Is not the destiny of everything unknown?
Not in vain, Sorrow, you go hourly
Into woman's heart as into your own home.

When was mercy shown the weak?
And who can justify his existence?
Cliffs of Leucadia, you are not the only
Preserver of some legend of sorrow!

O, voice of love and selflessness!
You will lead us to deception and woe.
Light of ecstasy, holy revelations,
Gifts of heaven—you are useless to us.

All is vanity! High callings,
The gush of feelings and the dream of joy,
And all the struggles, sacrifices, sufferings,
Things of earth—all these vanity."

The sighing stopped. And like a bright vision
He stands before the helpless girl,
And looking toward the lights of the heavens,
With the sorrowful blessing of love
He placed his hand on her head.

And surging like the pull of mighty waves,
The echoes of her feelings and sad thoughts
Are carried along before her
But more clearly, more sternly, and more fully:

"What do you seek, heedless young girl?
Look around at what the world frets over!
Devoting all its life to a phantom,
You do the same; find yourself an idol!

And clothe it with your reveries
And wait for happiness, stubborn child!
It will answer the soul's passion, the heart's

                                  outpourings

By being bored or by joking.

At times your love will be rewarded
With a distracted, hurried kiss.
You are a woman! Learn to control yourself,
Close your lips and chain your soul.

Hold back your passion and its sounds
Teach your tears not to flow.
You are a woman! Live without defenses,
Without caprice, without will, without hope.

Do not call the slaves of need, the blind sons of care
Into your secret world, the world of your heart:
With every day, new labors await them
They have no time for happiness and love.

But you must preserve the sacred visions
But you, in your deceived soul
Must learn how to keep a vow of perfect faith
In the disturbance of their pagan passions.

Do not try to know their fruitless freedom
Keep your undertakings safe from theirs;
Let people hurry and be noisy,
Don't ask what all the noise is for!
Go quietly, go to the wilderness again,
To the perfection of unrewarded labor;
Go once again to what was here today,
What will be here tomorrow and forever!

And at the end of the oppressive journey
Ask why there are so many wearying days,
Why the creator's orders are so stern
And why the lot of the powerless still harder."

V

About a week after the excursion to Ostankino, at the beginning of a hot day, Vera Vladimirovna and her daughter were drinking tea on their balcony in the shade of some thick trees covered with grayish dust. In front of the garden the wide white road glistened in the sunlight. The wind was making the light sand on the road swirl. On both sides one could see the sidewalk boundary posts lined up neatly one after the other. Opposite their house stood exactly the same kind of smart house with a balcony, flower garden, trees and a green gate. Both women had the notion that it was very early, that is about ten o'clock, and while taking their breakfast, they were enjoying what they imagined was nature and the morning. Cecily was paler and more silent than usual. In spite of herself, she felt strange and uneasy inside, a feeling she could not cope with. Her soul was so highly polished, her understanding so confused, her natural talents so overorganized and mutilated by the unsparing way she had been brought up that every problem of life embarrassed and terrified her. Her mother's lessons and moral teachings were about as useful to her in relation to life as are the endless commentaries of zealous scholars to Shakespeare and Dante. Once you have read them through, you won't understand even the clearest and simplest idea in the poet's creation any more. Her morals and intellect were improved upon as arbitrarily and thoroughly as were the poor trees in the gardens of Versailles when people were trimming them mercilessly into the shapes of columns, vases, spheroids or pyramids, so that they might represent anything other than trees. Nevertheless, mothers like Vera Vladimirovna most likely

43

understand something of the possible consequences of their method, because all of them are in an incredible hurry to get their perfected daughters off their hands and charge someone else with this dangerous responsibility that weighs down on them.

A fast-moving carriage thundered along the noisy street in front of the house and stopped at their entrance.

"It's Natalia Afanasievna," Cecily said, glancing up; and Natalia Afanasievna came in with Nadezhda Ivanovna.

"Bonjour, chère! You weren't expecting me so early, but I'm afraid of the heat. You know I have to cross the whole park to see you. I got up early today like country folk, *et me voilà*. What are you doing?"

"Nothing special," Vera Vladimirovna answered. "Cécile has not been quite well these past two days, but today she's better. And now today I am having a severe dizzy spell. And Olga?"

"Olga is well; she's in a big hurry to finish her rug for our lottery. By the way, how many tickets have you distributed?"

"Only twenty. I gave eight to Serge."

"Please try to give out the rest of them too. I still have about fifty, but today I'm giving half of them to Princess Alina. She's wonderful at distributing them. A propos, are you going to poor Madame Stentsova's funeral today?"

"Well, it seems I must," answered Vera Vladimirovna, "Yesterday Princess Anna Sergeevna said that even she was going. Only I don't know how I'll make it. I'm definitely so unwell today that I don't even have the strength to stand throughout the whole service. I think I won't go to the church but just sit in my carriage and go to the cemetery, out of respect for the old mother."

"Fine. I'll do the same thing. This morning I've a lot of necessary business to attend to. I won't make it to the church; I'll get there only at the end of the ceremony. So we can ride together. If you like, drop by for me; I'm on your way."

"Fine. What an unexpected death!"

"Yes, the poor woman was at the Princess' last evening party."

"Yes. I was talking to her there. How old was she?"

"About thirty-two, but she seemed older."

"What a pity! She was an extremely nice and kind woman. Her husband must be out of his mind with grief."

"No, her husband is quite in his mind," Madame Valitsky answered with a slight smile. "And he doesn't have too much to grieve over anyway; he wasn't very happy."

"Yes, so they say. But she loved him very much."

"Yes, she loved him after her own fashion, maybe too much. At least he himself made it clear that he would have liked to be loved a bit less."

"You mean he didn't succeed?" asked Vera Vladimirovna.

"It seems not, no matter how hard he tried."

Vera Vladimirovna remembered that Cecily was present and took advantage of the convenient opportunity to draw a moral lesson.

"For all the husband's faults," she pronounced in a stern voice, "the wife is guilty. Her duty is to know how to bind him to her and make him love virtue."

Madame Valitsky was naturally in complete agreement with this.

The conversation lasted a few minutes longer in a similar vein, and then Natalia Afanasievna stood up.

"Well, goodbye for now. I'm leaving Nadezhda Ivanovna with you. You can bring her back to me later on. *A tantôt.* And please don't be late; be at my place at two o'clock."

She left, and Nadezhda Ivanovna, as a result of her longtime habit of not being surprised that people disposed of her with such ease, as if she were an object loaned back and forth, took from her pocket a half-finished purse also

45

destined for the charitable lottery and began to crochet it.

The Park's appearance was changing little by little: the sidewalks were becoming more populated, the road noisier, the dust thicker and more plentiful. Carriages bowled along, dashing men galloped by on horseback, and attractive ladies walked on either side of the road to take advantage of the shade. Others sat on their balconies and terraces, under broad awnings. That whole conventional, arrogant world was coming to life.

Ordinary people were no longer visible; those who worked had gone home. Unless somewhere a peasant resting under a bush, hearing suddenly the unaccustomed thunder of wheels or the gallop of a horse, lifted up his head a little, looked around peacefully and lay down again, wondering silently to himself.

The time for morning visits had arrived. Two or three ladies and five or six men visited Vera Vladimirovna's drawing room; Dmitry Ivachinsky arrived, Prince Victor appeared as well. They began to speak again of the sudden death of Madame Stentsova and mourned the dead woman.

"She was not at all bad-looking," said Prince Victor.

"Her complexion was too dark," said Nadezhda Ivanovna.

The Prince looked at her with some surprise, not having expected the unseemly retort from this living piece of furniture, and continued lazily:

"Not at all bad-looking, remarkable eyes, only terribly boring."

"Quite an empty woman," said one lady, "I could never talk to her for more than ten minutes and even that was difficult."

"She was, unfortunately, an imprudent woman," Vera Vladimirovna answered, "and didn't know how to keep the love of her husband to whom she was indebted for her whole fortune."

"Not a very large fortune," Dmitry Ivachinsky

46

remarked, "six hundred souls."

"Including ones from Kostroma," added a fat gentleman who owned peasants from Tambov and Yaroslav.

"It's lucky that there are no children," another lady said. "Stentsov will probably marry again."

"Yes, and we have already guessed to whom," said the fat gentleman with an unbearably complicated smile.

As this conversation continued Cecily sat by the window at her lace-frame. Dmitry Ivachinsky got up from where he was sitting and drew near to that window, to Nadezhda Ivanovna who was sitting nearby, and began to say something to her, all the while looking fixedly and persistently at the empty stool near Cecily.

Not a single mother explains and every daughter understands such rhetoric. Cecily gently raised her head with a favorable, silent answer to the humble question, then lowered it sternly and in an unfriendly manner. Opposite her, leaning against the door to the balcony, stood Prince Victor with a barely perceptible smile and a disturbing glance. The obedient Dmitry remained behind Nadezhda Ivanovna's chair and the Prince slowly assumed a dignified manner, walked directly to the sacred stool and sat down on it without asking permission to do so. Cecily bent her blushing face to some flowers standing near her and, hesitating a long time in her choice, tore off a sprig of heliotrope. The Prince began to speak of the previous day's light comedy and of a coming horse race. Cecily could not possibly do anything but listen and answer. The Prince, while speaking, carelessly stretched out his hand to the lace-frame where Cecily was toying with the torn-off sprig and took it. Vera Vladimirovna, sitting quietly in her long armchiar, was unobserved following all his movements. The ladies present saw as artfully as she everything to which they were paying no attention, but all were sufficiently wise and knew that it befits a prudent mother to act with severity only with impoverished suitors and that the laws of the most refined conventionality are out of place with one who can give in exchange for a flower he has taken a half-million in yearly income.

After ten minutes or so the Prince yawned slightly, got up, bowed imperceptibly, went out and sped away in his foreign carriage, in his foreign clothes, with his foreign wit, leaving the crumpled sprig of heliotrope on the floor and the humiliated Dmitry next to Nadezhda Ivanovna.

Cecily from her window looked out after the stormy black horse carrying him away in a cloud of dust. Did she regret inwardly that Dmitry had no such equipage? Did she notice that her own Russian coachman decidedly did not stand comparison with the Prince's English groom? Did she think that all other women would envy the one among them who could fly past them in that fascinating creation of London "high fashion. . ."? She glanced up for only a minute and bent over her sewing.

In the drawing room a fairly lively argument was in progress:

"A most absurd wedding," someone said.

"She acted very cleverly," asserted one lady. "Their fortune was completely dissipated, the estate was supposed to be auctioned off. There was a mass of debts. She found herself a son-in-law who would restore and pay for everything."

"Monsieur Chardet!" answered one of the men in the group.

"Yes, it was Monsieur Chardet," she exclaimed. "He's really a very respectable man."

"But is he rich?"

"Of course. He has transacted some very profitable business. Sophia will be very happy with him."

"He gave her a marvelous emerald necklace," another lady said. "I saw it yesterday."

"It's still not a pleasant means of rescue."

"Pardon me, but you are behind the times. What do

48

aristocratic prejudices mean in such a case! Mésalliances are very much in fashion now. George Sand has lent a kind of charm to ordinary people."

"Are you really a follower of George Sand?" Dmitry Ivachinsky asked her with a smile.

"To a certain extent: I like the folk element a good deal."

"With the exception of their raw sheepskin coats," he remarked.

"Well, yes, of course. But in fact there are marvelous peasants; one can meet them with pleasure, only naturally not as guests in one's own house."

Meanwhile time passed. Vera Vladimirovna's drawing room grew empty.

"Cécile," she said, "I have to go to the funeral now. You stay here with Miss Stevenson. I may be returning late. I'll probably be spending the evening with Natalia Afanasevna at Madame Stentsova's mother's house and somewhere else as well. So don't wait up for me and go to bed at a decent hour. You are still not well. Goodbye, dear!"

Vera Vladimirovna went out with Nadezhda Ivanovna, and Cecily remained alone with Miss Stevenson, in other words, completely alone. She was decidedly not herself. She couldn't explain what was weighing on her spirit and she didn't try very hard. She didn't put to herself the only essential question, she didn't ask herself whether in fact she loved Dmitry Ivachinsky. According to her understanding there was no room for doubt about this. But she didn't know what she had to do, how to attain the fulfillment of her wishes, how to go about it. If she had been in any condition to understand that a true feeling cannot hesitate and waver, that from the moment consciousness becomes real and clear, action is equally clear and real because it has become a necessity and necessity knows no impediments; if she had been taught to look a truth in the face, if she could have guessed what it means to love. . . . But how was

Philosophy

49

this possible when not only feeling itself, not only an understanding of what it was, but the very word had always been kept remote from her and cast aside like a tainted thing. Everything strove to suppress all spiritual strength in her, to kill all inner life. And still her young heart was not able to unlearn to tremble, and still she could not renounce life and love, and her exacting, impatient soul was ready to embrace a cloud and a phantom instead of a heavenly being. — At present she vaguely and unconsciously sensed something false, but what and where? Whether in her inner or outer life she was not able to seek out and clarify. . . . Alas, all her life was only a long and uninterrupted lie!

Towards evening her slightly feverish condition grew worse. Miss Stevenson advised her to drink raspberry juice and lie down. She lay down. Incoherent thoughts wandered through her head. She remembered the ride to Ostankino and that morning and Prince Victor and that poor woman who had just been buried, who just a few days ago had been sitting before her, intense and happy. . . . It was getting late . . . she became lost in thought. For a long time she looked into the half-darkness of the bedroom; but the evening grew dark, the room began to disappear before her eyes, finally it did disappear, and a broad darkness fell . . . but something far off glimmered and grew light . . . and many faces and many fires were there . . . and meanwhile in the shadows, mysteriously hidden, *his* barely distinct breath drifted above her. . . .

And meanwhile a discordant noise was heard again,
The crowd pressed close within the dazzling rooms,
Wine flowed—the funeral feast progressed,
And the hum around the tables spread and grew.
And loud words took the place of toneless speech,
Smiles came to life, slander woke from sleep,
Worldly vanity, irresistible,

50

Knocked boldly even on the coffin's wood.

And there, in the distance, the moon came up;
And there, in the obscurity of night
The new grave shone black,
Already forgotten by the crowd.
And lime-trees, whispering among themselves
In a language no one understands,
Softly swayed their heads
In their secret anguish.
And the meadow was drenched
In heavy tears of dew,
And in the twilight mist
Two furrows gleamed white.
Near the grove two puffs of down
Drifted in the empty shade
Two voices merged, despondent,
With the murmuring leaves on the hill.

First Voice:
And you have crossed your arms in the coffin,
Leaving behind the noise of the world,
And all the struggles, all the partings,
All the strivings of the earth!
You too, poor thing, were searching for
A pure pearl in the sea of life
And you died in vain, sorrowfully,
Victim of a ruinous dream!

Second Voice:
And did she enter into this world
To live an empty life and die a useless death?
And is the blind loss of will not sinful,
And is the power of crazed thought not shameful?
What has she brought to life? where
                              is her life's work?

51

How can her soul be reconciled with the earth?
Did she look boldly into the face of fate?
Didn't she lie even to herself?
Didn't she lose heart at the power
of an inner summons?
Did she fulfill the task entrusted to her?
Did she go forth? Did she seek the word of life?
Was she stronger than her sorrow?

First Voice:
The yoke of earth's constraints
She did not bear on earth,
Did not doubt the doubtful,
Did not struggle in the fight.
She loved sorrowfully and passionately,
Believing in another's love,
And waited to the end in vain,
And hoped until the end.

Second Voice:
Why murmur against eternal laws?
Why not recognize the limits of the possible?
Groans are no substitute for holy labor,
Life is better than dreams and truth
higher than lies.
Who is to blame that she had not the strength
To face the path, measure its steepness,
Not to expect miracles, understand
people from the first
And count only on herself!
Why, meeting deception every day,
Did she not renounce false faith
And why in the ruinous alchemy of the soul
Did she squander its store of wealth?

First Voice:
Stronger than insult, stronger than deception
Was the sacred passion of love in her.
Her wound could not subside,
Her sad gift could not disappear.
Who knew in that falsely rigorous world
Where grief is shameful and a joke,
How inconsolably she wept,
Resigned, before God,
What sacrifices she made,
What questions filled her heart,
In how severe a storm her soul
After a long struggle was torn apart?
No! If one has searched obscurely
For something which in life cannot be found,
If after hundreds of deceptions
One still could keep a blessed hope intact,
And measure with his soul on earth
A surfeit of those superearthly powers,
One is not guilty because he has believed,
One is not guilty because he has loved.

VI

The day was drawing near that Vera Vladimirovna always celebrated—Cecily's birthday. This time, too, she had made various preparations to spend it as gaily as possible: a dinner, a concert, a *bal champêtre*, a supper—every possible thing that could be done was done, with great effort and at great expense. The gaiety of people of the highest circles is incredibly expensive. When Cecily woke up that day, she found her mother's gifts lying on her sofa: two charming dresses, one a dinner dress, the other an evening dress, and the most marvelous lace scarf, ordered from Paris. In the course of the morning she received approximately two dozen bouquets and three dozen notes from friends—all saying precisely the same thing, to which it was necessary to respond with precisely the same variations. Society women have attained the wondrous art of contriving thirty variations on a phrase which means nothing even the first time. Then Madame Valitsky arrived with her daughter (on that morning no other people were received). Cecily went into the garden with Olga to rest from her correspondence a bit. They settled into a corner where there was some shade and began to chatter away; they talked of twenty different subjects, and then Olga's voice grew lower and more secretive.

"Listen," she said, "you're killing Ivachinsky. He was so upset by your coolness yesterday that out of desperation he lost all night at cards at Ilichev's and almost went out of his mind."

"Who told you that?" Cecily asked.

"A cousin told it to Mama. He was there and saw Dmitry. You're really driving him to goodness knows what. He's becoming a gambler."

It was not Olga herself who was saying these things: it was her mother's prompting. Only Madame Valitsky knew the great power and naivete of female egotism; only Madame Valitsky knew how much more interesting to a woman a man becomes, and how much dearer, the moment she sees the possibility of changing him in her own fashion, reforming him from vice, saving him from destruction. The greater the danger, the deeper the abyss ready to swallow him, the more glorious is the triumph, the more tempting the success, the greater the pleasure in stretching out to the one who is perishing a saving hand, fragile and yet all-powerful. Madame Valitsky had decided that Cecily must become Dmitry's wife so that she would not somehow become the wife of Prince Victor, and Madame Valitsky proceeded toward her goal. And Olga, for her part, was also of a mind to keep the precious Prince for herself and did not trust Cecily too much in this respect. Although Olga was too young to know what levers to pull, she was clever enough to use them according to her mother's directions. In society's lexicon, this sort of move is called "adroit" or "clever."

Instead of answering, Cecily bowed her head and fell to thinking. But there wasn't much time to think that day; it was time to dress for dinner. Madame Valitsky and her daughter left, so that they too could dress and return in a couple of hours, and Cecily went to her room, called the maid and sat down at her dressing-table, loosening her black braids. She was so full of thoughts and day-dreams that she paid no attention to the hair-do Annushka was laboring over. Looking into her mirror, she thought only of what Olga had said. So she was capable of bringing Dmitry to desperation. A possibility always flattering and satisfying to a woman, and as a result of which she began to

56

await him with great impatience.

But however much these thoughts possessed her she could not help but be distracted, if only briefly, while putting on the splendid new dress. And indeed, when she was all ready and standing before her mirror, it presented such a picture of grace that, looking at it, she understood perfectly poor Dmitry's torments of the heart.

The dinner was, like all dinners of this sort, long and boring. Aside from Vera Vladimirovna's husband and two or three guests like him, who ate with great appetite, everyone was waiting for it to end—Cecily and Olga more than anyone, because Prince Victor and Dmitry were not expected until evening. Once dinner was over with, they could still have a few pleasant hours to themselves.

The time for the concert finally arrived. The guests, whose number had increased, pressed into the room and began listening very patiently to variations and fantasias, arias and duets, accompanied by the constant movement of chairs set down for new arrivals. An Italian duet sung by Olga and Cecily ended the concert. It was, of course, delightful, since it had been taken from the latest opera and, of course, it gave the listeners enormous delight. The entire three rows of toques and mob-caps in front of the pianos rippled. All the men, mercilessly squeezed into the corners and along the walls, clapped their hands in a storm of delight. Dmitry Ivachinsky, who had just come in the door, was so unsparing of himself that he tore his gloves to shreds. Prince Victor himself applauded more than when he had heard Grisi in Paris. The duet, in a word, produced a huge effect, after which they all dispersed into the garden with frank delight.

Cecily took Olga by the arm and ran with her toward her own room in order to escape the general thanks, comb her hair, and change for the ball. In the doorway stood Dmitry Ivachinsky. He bowed to her and whispered five or six words. Cecily nodded her head and passed swiftly by.

"Olga," she said, after running upstairs to her room and gazing at the dark waves of her hair in the mirror, "are you promised for the mazurka?"

"Since yesterday morning," Olga answered in a voice so content that one could have no doubt as to whom she was promised. "And you?"

"Since just a minute ago," Cecily said, even more content, throwing her marvelous scarf on the sofa.

She felt extraordinarily happy, somehow wildly and boldly happy. She gave herself over to new, engrossing feelings. She was dimly aware of certain unknown possibilities. The daughter of Eve was tasting the forbidden fruit. The young captive was breathing in free, fragrant, unfamiliar air and growing drunk on it. Vera Vladimirovna had never wished to admit such an eventuality. Those prudent, vigilant, cautious women never do. They rely totally on their maternal efforts. They are extremely consistent with their daughters. In place of the spirit they give them the letter, in place of live feeling a dead rule, in place of holy truth a preposterous lie. And they often manage through these clever, precautionary machinations to steer their daughters safely to what is called " a good match." Then their goal is attained. Then they leave her, confused, powerless, ignorant and uncomprehending, to God's will; and afterwards they sit down tranquilly to dinner and lie down to sleep. And this is the very same daughter whom at the age of six they could not bring themselves to leave alone in her room, lest she fall off a chair. But that was a matter of bodily injuries (blood is quite visible, physical pain is frightening), not of an obscure, mute pain of the spirit.

One could be consoled if it were only bad mothers that acted like this. There are not many bad mothers. But it is the very best mothers who do it and will go on doing it forever. And all these bringers-up were young once, were brought up in the same way! Were they really so satisfied with their own lives and with themselves that they are happy

58

to renew the experience with their children? Is all this absurdity as long-lived as those reptiles which continue to exist after they are cut into pieces? Didn't these poor women weep? Didn't they blame themselves and other people? Didn't they look for help in vain? Didn't they feel the meaninglessness of the support given them? Didn't they recognize the bitter fruit of this lie?

But many of them, perhaps, did not! There are incredible cases and strange exceptions. There are examples of people falling from the third floor onto the pavement and remaining unharmed; then why not give one's daughter, too, a shove?

And it must be said, too, that so much is forgotten in life, the years change and reshape us so strangely! So many young, inspired dreamers in time become tax-farmers and distillers. So many carefree young idlers become owners of Siberian gold mines. So many flighty scoundrels become merciless punishers of every kind of passion. Time is a strange force!

When the friends came downstairs together in their ball gowns and appeared among the guests, they were truly beautiful. Olga, in a white dress of exceedingly expensive simplicity, with cornflowers in her long blond curls, was astonishingly lovely; but Cecily, who was also all in white, with a crown of white roses set over her proud black braids, was even lovelier. Olga was still searching for something; Cecily had already found it. Olga glowed with hope; Cecily shone with victory. In her face, her smile, her whole glance, in every movement there was something too beautiful for good form, something splendidly ravishing, a sort of victory of Poltava. And this was only the shadow of love! But love is so inexpressibly exciting that even its shadow is full of charm and better than anything else in the world.

The weather was most propitious. The starry night wafted a marvelous life-giving warmth. The ball, or rustic ball, as it was called, was set up on the model of a certain Parisian party given not long before and quite in the new fashion. The carefully rolled courtyard in front of the house entrance served as a ballroom. It was tightly encircled by a double row of laurels and orange-trees and tall rare flowers. Among the branches gas lamps were burning, pouring their bright light onto the whole scene. The adjacent garden was also illuminated, but more dimly, with small flames in translucent porcelain globes and alabaster vases. It had been transformed into a drawing room, study tables and a buffet. Opulent furniture was artfully arranged throughout. Tea-tables were standing under fragrant shrubs. Pyramids of fruit rose in the middle of multicolored dahlias and beautiful camellias composed into luxuriant bunches. Mysterious lights glowed fantastically through the dark green. All this was indeed surprisingly pleasant.

From behind a thick mass of acacias an invisible orchestra started to play; the ball had begun. Thanks to that unusual setting and the attractive novelty of it all, the decorous, indolent aristocratic company came unexpectedly to life. Dances followed swiftly one after the other. At times light feminine laughter was heard in the night air. Everything was movement, noise and gaiety. The tranquil stars looked down from their heights, a few old trees stood in sullen silence, gloomy and motionless among the crowd.

Time passed. The dances continued. Cecily, always quickly tired, felt no fatigue that evening. A new, inexplicable existence was growing in her. One of those rich hours of life had struck when the heart is so full of itself that no happiness is capable of taking it by surprise. At that moment a miracle would have seemed natural and ordinary to her: she would not even have noticed it. If one of those shining stars had fallen to earth before her, she would have simply pushed it away with her foot.

Providence sometimes bestows such moments on earthly existence!

It was close to midnight. The party, as always happens around this time, reached its most brilliant moment. Din and motion were everywhere. Everywhere through the greenery glimmered dresses of different colors, floating scarves, glittering bracelets on white arms. Everywhere voices were heard; the jokes, mockery, compliments, slander, vulgarity of some, the wit of others, the coquetry of still others—all mixed and blended into one general sound of voices. From its fathomless darkness, the night sky shone strangely above this turmoil. Those drawing room speeches, those empty words sounded somehow insolent in the dark infinity; the worldly, false, over-civilized mode of life made a sinful, sacrilegious noise in God's free expanse.

After many quadrilles Olga, Cecily and another young girl sat down to rest, the three of them on a small divan in a cosy half-hidden corner of the garden. Dmitry Ivachinsky came up to them and began to talk with the third girl; she laughed and answered him animatedly. Suddenly the mazurka started up. Olga took her neighbor who had been talking with Dmitry by the hand and ran off with her. Cecily also stood up, took a couple of steps, looked around and stopped. For a minute she was alone with Ivachinsky.

"Dmitry Andreevich," she said suddenly, with a charming blush," I have to ask you something; don't play cards as you did yesterday at Ilichev's. You will promise, won't you? You won't gamble any more?"

"I won't," he answered, "if you'll give me that flower you tore off your bouquet and are holding in your hand."

The mazurka thundered louder. Cecily flitted through the garden, but the flower fell from her hands onto the path.

She stopped for a second, at the turning of the path: did she really have to look, to know whether it had been found? It was lying in Dmitry's hand, and he was following behind her. She stretched out her own hand a little with the insincere intention of taking it back, but her look was more honest than her hand. There was no one in the garden. Dmitry grasped her outstretched fingers and kissed them swiftly.

Two minutes later she began dancing the mazurka with him and slipped into the bright circle, surrounded by chairs, among the crowd of onlookers. But who among them could see how tenderly that trembling little hand, which had been kissed for the first time, was grasped?

It was the same simple story once again, old and forever new! It was true that Dmitry was captivated with Cecily. The magnetism of others' opinions always had an astonishing effect on him. Seeing her that evening so dazzling and so surrounded, he could not fail to be satisfied with her, and far more satisfied with himself. He was one of those weak creatures who grow drunk on success. At that moment he was no longer merely calculating: he saw himself placed higher than all the rest by Cecily, higher even than Prince Victor, the arrogant object of his secret envy; and his head began to turn. Inside him there started up youth's wildness and its irresistible burst of passion, as at the height of battle, when the warrior rushes blindly forward to tear the standard from the enemy ranks at any cost. This actually resembled love. It was, perhaps, mixed with some attraction of the heart as well, but this was only that ruthless masculine feeling which, if the woman inspiring him had committed some awkwardness, had worn some ugly hairdo or unfashionable hat, could at any moment change into fierce malice.

But one could lay odds that Cecily was incapable of committing the slightest awkwardness and would always be perfectly dressed and coiffed.

The mazurka ended at last. Supper was waiting on various tables, large and small, placed about the garden. Cecily and Dmitry sat as far as they could from one another. They now intentionally kept their distance; they were already two conspirators hiding their association.

The party was coming to a close. Coaches and carriages were brought round. As Madame Valitsky had requested, Dmitry found her carriage and accompanied her to it. While they were walking he bent towards her a little and whispered in a conspiratorial voice:

"Let me visit you tomorrow morning, Natalia Afanasevna. I'm going to ask you to do me an important service."

"I'll be waiting with great pleasure," she answered. "Come about one."

The lackey opened the doors of the carriage. Madame Valitsky sat down feeling almost as lively and happy as her daughter.

The short summer night was already turning pale by the time the guests had all left. It may be said that everyone, or nearly everyone at least, was satisfied. They had rushed about, danced, made noise and amused themselves to exhaustion. For her part, Vera Vladimirovna lay down to sleep quite satisfied. Her party had been a complete success, and Prince Victor had looked at Cecily often and had stated at two different times that she was extremely lovely. Madame Valitsky also lay down to sleep very satisfied: just one more little push was needed to get that dangerous Cecily out of the way. Olga lay down to sleep even more satisfied: the Prince had talked a lot of nonsense to her during the mazurka and had remarked that her dress was exceptionally becoming. Dmitry could not be dissatisfied: his egotism was still in full carouse and, as he fell asleep, he felt inwardly victorious. Prince Victor always went to sleep completely satisfied with himself and with others. Finally, even poor Nadezhda Ivanovna, who never succeeded in anything, who never arranged anything or expected anything, whom no one danced with or spoke to—even she fell asleep satisfied, for no reason at all.

But Cecily lay down to sleep with that abounding happiness which sometimes fills an eighteen-year-old heart for

63

a moment, and which is so alive that in quiet and solitude one becomes almost ill with it. She could not think, but there was a turmoil in her chest, and fantasies began. Her closed eyes still saw the ball, the bright-colored crowd and the illuminated garden. And her drowsing consciousness grew inexplicably somber with some unaccountable feeling. Happy, she sighed sorrowfully, not knowing why. And comfortingly, a languorous drowsiness descended on her. It seemed as if echoes of the orchestra were carrying through the hush—distant, half-sorrowful harmonies, now stopping, now starting up again, and melting into strange talk, mysterious conversations, marvelous, wished-for sounds, *his* call, into *his* greeting:

"The far-off star
Has long been flaming;
Long have I waited,
The hour goes by.
Languishing in an evil dream
In this strange land,
Awake, beloved,
In your own country;
Among the victorious
Sacred things of night,
Leave the deception
Of material worry."

Sad is the smile on his lips,
His words flow more gently:
"O, eternal error of the heart,
How early you have grown close to her!
How soon the voice of bold convictions
Has been awakened in her!
How many painful revelations,
How many sorrows lie ahead!
How life will try in vain to disenchant

64

Her soul to the very end!
Alas! There in the world all is unclear,
There all is blind and false raving!
With dark, mute thought, you
Will search there for me alone:
It is in me your soul believes,
Me that you love, not him.
But in the midst of changing vanity
In your routine of every day,
I will remain an unclear sadness,
A dream of the heart unrealized.
And sensing light in the depths of gloom,
Trusting in an unearthly secret,
You will travel from ghost to ghost,
From one sorrow to another.
In all that will be dear to your heart,
In all you will see the same lie;
You have loved the infinite,
You wait for the immeasurable.
It is not life, o fateful thirsting,
That will assuage your pain!
You will have another future,
Other streams of life.
Thus let your fate turn out a bitter one,
The bright paradise of hopes vanish!
Get used to a difficult path
And learn the strength of the weak.
Understand that the Lord's commandments
Have doomed you, defenseless ones,
To unconditional patience
To a task higher than that on earth.
Learn, as a wife, the suffering of a wife,
Know that, submissive, she
Must not seek the path
To her own dreams, her own desires;
That her heart protests in vain,

That her duty is implacable,
That all her soul is in his power,
That even her thoughts are fettered.
Prepare all the strength of youth
For mute tears, for an obscure struggle,
And may the heavenly father give you
An unconquerable love!"

VII

On the following morning, before noon, Natalia Afanasevna was sitting on her terrace. On the little table in
front of her stood a cup of chocolate and the latest of the
countless works of Alexandre Dumas; but the cup of delicious beverage remained full and the book by the absorb-
ing storyteller unopened. Madame Valitsky was in no
mood for chocolate or for stories just now: she herself was
preparing the dénouement to the prologue of a certain real-
life novel of great interest to her. She leaned her elbows
meditatively on her soft armchair, then took a watch from
under the sash of her peignoir and cast a momentary
glance at it, then from time to time got up, walked to one
side of the terrace, from where she could see the broad
avenue of the park and looked through her lorgnette into
the dusty distance. Returning discontented to her armchair
for the third or fourth time, she began to toy impatiently
with the little mother-of-pearl handled knife lying on the
book.

Steps were heard. Nadezhda Ivanovna appeared on
the terrace, very red and tired.

"Where have you been?" asked Natalia Afanasevna.

"Walking with Olga almost halfway around the park.
We're all tired out."

"Why do you go walking in the heat? Where is Olga?"

"She went with Miss Jeffries to her room. As we were
coming back we met some young people—Sofia Chardet
and her husband. They were in a carriage."

"Indeed?"

"Yes, she was wearing a marvelous cloak."

"Have you sent to find out about Katerina Vasilevna's health?"

"Yes; they still haven't returned with the answer."

Again Madame Valitsky glanced at her watch. While continuing to ask empty questions out loud, inwardly she was asking herself completely different uneasy ones: "Did he really make up his mind and then decide not to come? . . . Impossible. How shall I manage Vera Vladimirovna? She won't agree: it's not a fantastic match. Will I really not be able to handle this? I have to think up something! But what?"

A swift droshky pulled up with a clatter and stopped. It was Dmitry.

At that exact moment, as if it were called forth by the noise of the wheels, Madame Valitsky was struck with a sudden, completely unexpected, bold and magnificent idea.

"Nadezhda Ivanovna," she said hurriedly, "please order them to harness up the carriage for me, and leave me alone with Ivachinsky. I have to talk over some business with him. Tell them not to receive any visitors. And not to come in to announce when the carriage is ready; I will ring for it myself. Go on now."

The obedient Nadezhda Ivanovna, fulfilling her almost daily duty, went out, and Dmitry Ivachinsky came in.

Madame Valitsky stretched out her hand to him in a friendly manner.

"Natalia Afanasevna," he said, "I have come to you with a most important request."

"I'm ready to do everything possible," she interrupted approvingly.

"It's a question of my life's happiness," he continued. "I am speaking to you directly and without rehearsal: I love Cecily Alexandrovna. I fell in love with her long ago; I have been hiding it for more than a year. But I can hide it no longer."

Dmitry was always carried away by his own words. One could say that he did not control them but rather the opposite. From this fact there sometimes resulted something similar to lying.

"I guessed your secret long ago," Natalia Afanasevna answered in her kindly voice.

"I beg you," he added, "help me to reach this happiness! Take it upon yourself to convey my request to Vera Vladimirovna. Try to win her over. Be my providence."

"Are you sure that Cecily loves you?" she asked.

"I have reason to assume it," he answered with a smile which gave a measure of his mind.

"It seemed so to me; but you see, Dmitry Andreevich, this whole business is very difficult. Let's speak openly with one another. There's an impediment here: Prince Victor. . . ."

"Prince Victor!" Dmitry burst out with proud scorn, not having the strength to refrain from the pleasure of pronouncing this name in such a tone for the first time.

"Yes, Prince Victor, although I am completely convinced that he has never thought seriously about Cecily as a bride for himself. . . ."

"He may have thought about her," Dmitry interrupted suddenly with a self-sufficient little joke, "but she has certainly not thought about him."

Madame Valitsky assumed her well-known expression which might mean anything at all, and continued:

"Perhaps, but he flirts with her all the same, and her mother hopes that a wedding will follow from this. His huge fortune tempts her against her will. I, for my part, have never thought of seeking wealth in choosing a husband for Olga, but Vera Vladimirovna is of another mind on that subject. I don't know if I can be of use to you in this business."

"Natalia Afanasevna! Be merciful! Don't refuse me

69

your aid. You alone can arrange it all. You are so close to Vera Vladimirovna. Convince her to agree to our happiness! This love is mutual. Cecily will be unhappy with some other husband as I will be with some other wife. Vera Vladimirovna truly does not wish her daughter to be miserable, nor would you. Wouldn't you really agree joyfully in such an instance if it were a question of Olga Alexeevna?"

"Fool!" Natalia Afanasevna was thinking.

"I cannot judge others by myself," she said sweetly, "and have no right to demand that they share my feelings and opinions. I have different conceptions of life's happiness and in such circumstances I would naturally not hesitate for a moment if I were in Vera Vladimirovna's place. But I am afraid that she is not like me in this respect. On the other hand I sincerely wish you success. But in order to attain it you must go about things extremely cautiously. You see I am of course very friendly with Vera Vladimirovna, but I have almost no influence over her. In order to put forth your proposition to her, we have to find someone whose opinion might influence her, someone who might command her respect. Let me think, . . . well, yes, who better? . . . Only will she do it?"

"Who is it?" Dmitry asked.

"None other than Princess Anna Sergeevna, Prince Victor's mother. Her request will carry a good deal of weight, and success would almost be guaranteed. Only it will be difficult to persuade her; you do not know her very well."

"But you know her very well, Natalia Afanasevna. Can't you ask her?"

"Yes, perhaps she won't say no to me. By the way, she loves to arrange weddings. Let us try! I want to justify fully your faith in me. Would you like me to take you to her right now so that I may try to ask it of her?"

"Natalia Afanasevna, I'm inexpressibly grateful to you. How kind you are!"

70

"I'm always sincerely happy to do a service to my friends," she said, "especially such an important service. It's a question of your happiness; I will do my utmost."

She rang; a manservant entered.

"My carriage in ten minutes," ordered Natalia Afanasevna. "Wait for me here," she continued, turning to Ivachinsky, "I'll be ready in a minute."

Indeed, she returned in a very short time, dressed and wearing a hat, and the carriage was brought around so soon that it might have been possible to guess that it was already standing harnessed and ready. Madame Valitsky and Dmitry sat down in it and rode to see Princess Anna Sergeevna.

On the way, Natalia Afanasevna, leaning back in the corner of the carriage, kept silent or distractedly answered Ivachinsky's words. The idea whose consequences she was already enacting was still lying obscure and undeveloped in her. This had been a sudden flash of light, one of those strokes of genius which never deceive us, however unreal and strange they may appear: you believe in success, not yet seeing its possibility, not yet understanding its realization. Now she was thinking everything through, clarifying all details, preparing the whole scene in her head, and she understood more and more that the affair would run smoothly, that the unbelievable would happen, that the particular occasion would not change, that no circumstances, no grain of sand would hinder its success. This success was hanging by a thread and would be destroyed by a single word; but Madame Valitsky had a presentiment that the thread would not break, that the word would not be spoken. This was the sixth sense of the intriguer, similar to the clairvoyance of the great.

They arrived, they were announced, they were received. The old princess was very busy with the inspection and selection of new material for dresses. But for Madame Valitsky's sake she cut short these profound talks and deliberations with a French Mademoiselle who was spreading out enticing goods before her, and, sending her away, she ordered her to return with them that evening, so that she could judge the effect of the materials by candlelight. Then she turned with a greeting to Natalia Afanasevna.

"Princess!" the latter began. "Knowing how kind you are, I took the liberty of bringing you a young man to whose happiness you can contribute. I was convinced in advance that you would not refuse."

"Delighted," muttered the Princess, not yet understanding and not recognizing Ivachinsky.

"Dmitry Andreevich Ivachinsky," said Madame Valitsky, introducing him. "You have met him."

"Delighted," the Princess repeated haughtily.

"Permit me to go into your study with you," Natalia Afanasevna continued. "I'll explain the reason for our visit in five minutes. I know that you are always glad of the occasion to do a good deed. Wait here in the meantime, Dmitry Andreevich."

She went into the study with the Princess who, to tell the truth, did not have such a great weakness for good deeds and favors as Madame Valitsky was convinced she had. But it is very hard to contradict such assurances and convictions; for the Princess it was even harder.

Princess Anna Sergeevna—God knows by what revelation—somehow surmised that in order to be a complete woman, it was fitting to add to wealth some other ingredient. Meanwhile, profoundly despising intellectual abilities and talents (which always seemed to her to be signs of something plebeian), having long since lost her former claim to eminence—beauty, understanding once again at her age that it was no longer a great virtue to be virtuous, she decided in her old age to be kind. This came at an unbelievably great cost to her egotistical nature, but she persisted and in fact was finally reputed to be kind to an impossible degree. Making use of this fact, it was very easy for Madame Valitsky to convince her, although at the outset the Princess did not even understand very well why she should play such a part with this Ivachinsky and go out and make a match for him. But Natalia Afanasevna was a past master at such moments: once she was alone with the Princess, she explained the whole matter to her perfectly and made her understand.

"You see, Princess, these poor children love one another passionately, but Vera Vladimirovna is looking for a brilliant match for her daughter, and the young man is not wealthy."

"Not everyone can be wealthy," the Princess very justly remarked.

"Completely true! But in any case Vera Vladimirovna does not wish Cecily to marry him. But she esteems and respects you to such an extent. . . ."

"The Princess' face was saying: I should think she would respect me!

"Your opinion," the advocate continued, "carries such weight that she probably will agree if you will only have a chat with her on this subject. You understand that for her to refuse you would be awkward."

"Of course," the Princess agreed.

"And so, you will ride over and sacrifice an hour in order to arrange the happiness of two hearts and save them from despair. I didn't doubt for a minute your readiness to fulfill my request."

"All right," the Princess answered, "I will leave immediately: one should not postpone a good deed."

"I guessed right about you," Natalia Afanasevna said. "But one more thing: you understand better than anyone how to make use of people's weaknesses in such instances." (Madame Valitsky, saying this, was truly inimitable.) "You know how Vera Vladimirovna is proud of her maternal perspicacity, and in fact she follows in a quite extraordinary fashion all the feelings and actions of her daughter.

73

She would be extremely insulted if you were to speak to her of this mutual love as of an event unknown to her, and even if you considered it necessary to mention the young man's name. It is understood that you will only hint to her about him in order not to insult her self-esteem. She will understand you at your very first words and will be very content to show you that she has understood and that nothing concerning Cecily can be hidden from her. What can you do? She is such a kind woman that one can forgive her this small bit of maternal vanity."

"Naturally," said the Princess, "and I will try to spare her."

"You are always so tactful," Madame Valitsky continued, "and know so well how to act with everyone! You know that in order to win over Vera Vladimirovna, one should not give her advice; she doesn't like it."

"I know," answered the Princess. "I will simply tell her that I have taken it upon myself to seek her consent."

"Exactly," said Natalia Afanasevna.

They came out together into the drawing room, where the impatient Dmitry was waiting. The Princess accepted the eloquent outpourings of his gratitude and ordered her carriage.

"Don't worry," she repeated, seating herself in it, "I will arrange everything and will send someone to tell you."

"I am sure, Princess," Natalia Afanasevna replied, "that you will act with extraordinary skill and will forget nothing that might lead to our goal. You have a knowledge of the heart."

With this the Princess set forth, already very satisfied with her own magnanimous selflessness, which drove her to ride out into the very heat of day, across almost the whole park, for another's benefit. And Natalia Afanasevna sat down again with Dmitry in her carriage and could not help pronouncing somewhat inspiredly:

"Home!"

Vera Vladimirovna was ready to set forth on her usual visits when Princess Anna Sergeevna's arrival was announced to her. This was an unusual event: the Princess rarely went out in the morning, and, having spent the whole previous evening at Vera Vladimirovna's house, she surprised her very much by appearing again on the following day. Here was something to wonder about. Vera Vladimirovna rushed to meet her and asked her to sit down.

"I have not come to you today on a simple visit," the Princess began. "I have taken upon myself a rather delicate business: I have been entrusted with making a proposal to you. . . ."

She stopped in order to take a pinch of snuff. Vera Vladimirovna shuddered inwardly as if galvanized by a shock. She dared not yet rejoice.

"The proposal is about Cecily," the Princess continued slowly. "You probably understand whom it concerns."

Vera Vladimirovna could not refrain from rejoicing.

"You probably noticed yesterday," the Princess added and took another pinch of snuff.

"I," Vera Vladimirovna said. "Indeed I did notice."

How could she not acknowledge this? She had in fact so vigilantly followed all the words and steps of Prince Victor in the course of the previous evening!

"Yes," the Princess added, "even I saw something too." (This would have demonstrated an incredible ability to see, because the Princess had spent nearly the whole evening at the card table, in a special room.) "Of course," she continued, "you have already guessed about Cecily's love as well!"

If this had come from anyone else, Vera Vladimirovna would have been extremely insulted by even the supposition that Cecily secretly loved someone. But the mother of Prince Victor was herself saying this. It was impossible for Vera Vladimirovna to contradict her in this. And besides it was no longer a question of taking offense.

75

"A loving mother always guesses all her daughter's movements of the heart," she exclaimed with feeling, barely hiding her triumphant bliss.

"I think," said the Princess, "that you have nothing against this."

Had her words been chosen by Madame Valitsky herself they could not have coincided better with the aims of the latter. One may pity the bold arranger of this scene that she did not witness it.

"I never wanted to hamper Cecily," the tender mother answered. "She made her choice freely. Her upbringing was a guarantee to me that this choice would be approved by me."

"I assumed so," the Princess said, "and I was convinced that you would not oppose this mutual love. And so, you agree?"

"Princess," Vera Vladimirovna answered, yielding to a very real temptation to make use of this auspicious moment, which allowed her to become with impunity a woman magnanimous and stoical, "I did not have wealth in mind for Cecily. I only wanted her to find a husband with qualities of soul and with a warm heart, a noble man in the true sense of the word. My wishes have been fulfilled; God has heard my prayer!"

"And so," the Princess said, still managing the conversation, "I may go home with a satisfactory answer? You agree?"

"I agree with sincere joy," Vera Vladimirovna assured her. "I could not wish for a better husband for my daughter. I know that she will be happy."

"Naturally," said the Princess, "you are completely right. Money does not buy happiness."

"Could she want to deprive her son of his inheritance?" the frightened Vera Vladimirovna was thinking.

"Love endures all things," continued the Princess, having recourse again to her golden snuffbox. "Your Cecily

76

will joyfully sacrifice empty superfluity and a few trivial habits. You knew so well how to develop her reason; even a moderate lot will satisfy her."

"What is this? What is this? . . ." the poor Vera Vladimirovna was thinking. "Lord, what does this mean? . . . Is she herself undertaking to remarry? The estate is indeed hers alone. . . ."

She glanced at the Princess. It was difficult to make such a supposition.

"And so," the Princess said, getting up, "I will go home to console the young man who impatiently awaits an answer. I am very happy for him. He has pleaded with me for so long that I could not refuse undertaking to speak to you about his proposal, although at first this even seemed to me not quite apropos. Well, thank God! A task completed. And he, poor man, feared a refusal. But I knew that you would agree. You are such a good mother. And he, it seems, is a very respectable man. He has good acquaintances. He can enter any profitable career, find patronage and make his way in life. I will tell Victor to help him. Well, then, goodbye."

Vera Vladimirovna was now completely in the dark. "So it isn't Prince Victor at all?" she asked herself with despair. "Well, who is it then? . . ."

But it was impossible to make inquiries about the name of the man to whom she had agreed to give her daughter.

Embarrassed, she looked for a possibility of salvation and didn't find it; in her mind all was confusion. Then it seemed the means appeared to her for an instant and she grasped at it with the eagerness of a dying person.

"Excuse me, Princess," she said. "Haven't we been in too much of a hurry in this? I must have a serious talk with Cecily."

"Her love is known to you," the Princess answered. "There is nothing to ask her."

77

"Of course . . . but even so . . . this is such an important step that a young girl must think it over thoroughly; it's so easy to make a mistake!"

"You were just saying that you could not wish for a better husband for Cecily."

"Of course . . . I am convinced . . . still . . . allow me to ask her. . . ."

The unhappy Vera Vladimirovna was becoming completely lost.

"If you please," said the Princess, "speak with her, although this seems to me completely unnecessary. She will surely be ready to marry the man she loves. Goodbye."

Vera Vladimirovna was saved. She could settle accounts with Cecily, she could learn her secret, forbid her to think about this man of no means, annihilate this stupid love and find some pretext, some excuse to refuse. She was, of course, an exceedingly kind mother, she was always ready to fulfill the whims and desires of her daughter; but this was an altogether different matter, this was not a joke.

Swiftly grasping all this, somewhat reassured, she escorted the Princess out.

Madame Valitsky's brilliant plan had not succeeded, she had lost the affair in spite of her firm faith in success. In order that this faith might not deceive her, it was now necessary for some completely extraneous, unforeseen circumstance to present itself.

The circumstance appeared.

It could not have been otherwise! Napoleon was not killed by an infernal machine because a woman took it into her head to wear a different shawl.*

Madame Valitsky found her lucky star in that moment. The Princess, accompanied by Vera Vladimirovna,

---

*A reference to the assassination attempt on the rue Saint-Nicaise on the 24th of December, 1800.

was walking toward the door. This door opened and Cecily entered in a cloak and hat, ready to ride with her mother.

"Well here she is!" exclaimed the Princess. "We shall ask her immediately. Listen, *ma chère enfant*, Ivachinsky is asking for your hand in marriage, your mother agrees; do you wish to marry him?"

Cecily blushed, grew pale again and said in happy confusion, "If Mama agrees, I will be happy to!"

"There, you see," the Princess joined in, "I was right. The poor children! Well, now everything is all right. I will send someone to tell him right away."

Vera Vladimirovna could not speak, could barely even understand.

The door opened again. Madame Valitsky and Olga appeared as if called forth at this decisive moment. Her instinct had guided her as surely as the raven points its way to carrion.

No sooner had she entered than she was completely at ease: at one glance she could guess everything.

"Congratulate Cecily," the Princess told her. "She is Ivachinsky's fiancée."

Olga hugged her best friend; Madame Valitsky clasped her good friend's hand with great feeling.

"You are a happy mother!" she told her.

Vera Vladimirovna began to cry.

The kind Princess sent her carriage for Dmitry. He arrived. Everything followed the usual order. Everyone was very moved, especially Natalia Afanasevna. Even Vera Vladimirovna's husband came home. Madame Valitsky, upon meeting him, immediately informed him of what had happened and that the only thing lacking was his consent. He consented and gave his daughter his blessing.

Vera Vladimirovna shuddered with sudden vexation at herself: in her confusion she had forgotton about her husband! He might have been a means of salvation if he had seemed not to want to give Cecily in marriage to Iva-chinsky. Now it was already too late to catch at this straw.

The Princess showered blessings and praises. She let it be known that she was very content with her morning and named herself as sponsor at the wedding.

Dmitry Ivachinsky stayed to dine and entered into all the rights of the fiancé. Vera Vladimirovna was, like all women of good society, sufficiently educated and polished to assume if necessary an air in no way corresponding to her inner feelings and was able even here to preserve excel-lently all the proprieties. For Cecily this day went by in joyful agitation; she could hardly believe in the truth of what had happened.

So she was really Dmitry's fiancée? The obstacles which were frightening her had vanished. All the difficul-ties had been smoothed over. She could touch her dream come true.

The evening went by extraordinarily rapidly. It was already late when Vera Vladimirovna sent Dmitry home.

Weary with happiness, Cecily entered her room. Me-chanically she lay down with a single thought, an ecstatic one. An atmosphere of peaceful happiness abundantly sur-rounded her and gave her life. Each thought caressed, each feeling lulled. . . .

Her quiet smile met the dream which was growing nearer. . . . It already wafted above her. . . .

And far away there were so many wonderful visions, bright blessings. . . .

And the wind barely whispers, barely blowing;
Through the mist of branches the moon looks on;
And the unending avenue of trees
Is full of the thick twilight.

Who, standing deep within,
Is seen briefly through the moonlit garden?

The mute shadow comes closer, blackly,
The starry glance shines brighter.

"Yes, I know, you are coming again;
Again you are looking into my heart;
Again your word comes forth,
Shatters my youthful dreams.

Sorrowful force, you always turn
My happiness to lies;
Like a flame glowing in a censer,
You light a ray of thought in me.

Leave me alone, stern spirit!
You grow sadder and gloomier;
I fear your revelations,
Your pitiless love.

Let me instruct my soul
For its daily, trivial fate:
I do not wish to foresee more,
No more do I wish to know!

Why do you tear in vain
Its mute prisoner from the world,
And teach an earthly being
To live without an earthly idol.

Should we really walk the path
Of earth so anxiously and so in vain,
Love only what is impossible,
Only believe in what is far away?

Why could you not leave the heart
A brief day of deception?
Why give me this ruinous lesson

In advance, so early?"

"In order that you might look out
Where fateful eternity awaits;
That you might understand something other
Than that series of empty cares.

In order that the light of the soul
Might not go out in the dark of earth;
In order that you not commit
Sacrilege upon yourself.

Arise out of the dust of life!
Calm the confusion in your heart!
Look without fear, immortal soul,
Into the face of truth!

Understand that all desires are vain,
That life is a series of losses,
That its sacrifices have no recompense,
That its sufferings have no reward.

And feel that within you there is something
Inexplicable at present,
Higher than any estimate,
And any blessings, any losses!"

VIII

Following that memorable morning which so suddenly decided Cecily's fate, everything around her changed and was enlivened, as usually happens in the house of a bride-to-be. The days went by swiftly one after the other, so filled up that they became completely empty. The ardent bridegroom, as is the custom, pleaded to hasten the wedding date; the prudent mother postponed it, asking for the time necessary for preparations. Vera Vladimirovna, seeing that nothing could be done anymore, proved that she was a very clever woman. She decided, to spite her foes and her friends, to be completely satisfied with this marriage and, using the framework in which she stood, to place very profitably in it the greater part of her virtues: unselfishness, magnanimousness, maternal love, and so forth and so on, so that she might have the pleasure of speaking fine phrases and receiving touching praise.

The house was invaded by merchants, shop-assistants, upholsterers, Tatars, Swedes,* milliners. Samples, parcels, hatboxes, packages were lying everywhere. There was no end to congratulatory visits; excursions, dinners, evening parties succeeded one another. All that vain futile motion of society life was sped up to the point of dizzying action. The lively tension, the gay noise surrounding a bride involuntarily calls to mind the deafening music and beating of the drum by which soldiers are led into deadly combat. So little time remained for the necessary arrangements. One

---

*These nationalities, along with other foreigners, were the tradespeople of Moscow and lived in special areas of town.

had to worry about details of such consequence, look over so many fashion magazines, choose so many different materials and fabrics of all sorts, talk so frequently with diamond merchants and goldsmiths, measure so many dresses, peignoirs, cloaks, shawls, hats, mob-caps and head-dresses, in a word, be so occupied with essential matters that not one free minute remained to muse idly upon any other thing.

And what and why was there anything to muse about, especially for Cecily? Her desires had been fulfilled, her secret dreams realized. Around her all was bright and beautiful. She had reached those enchanting hours of life when the curtain on a marvelous future near-at-hand slowly rises minute by minute, letting the young girl's glance peer in for a moment, her sensitive heart tremble joyfully. And all was so new for her, so unexpected, so unheard of. This entire world in which she suddenly found herself had always until now been kept secret from her, carefully put to the side and hidden, so that her understanding could not imagine a comparison with anything similar, and she had to consider herself some kind of blessed magnificent exception to the general order. Dmitry, moreover, did not modify the customary habits of fiancés and as innocently and goodheartedly as all of them led this ignorant, gullible soul from deception to deception, from delusion to delusion, one more consoling and charming than the other. For the lies of a watchful mother he substituted the lies of a tender lover, saving the inexorable truth for the dicta of a stern husband. Wherever one looked, everywhere pleasing and flattery, merry faces and friendly words were met with. What was there here to think over and contemplate? Precisely nothing. Everything was presented in a fine light; Cecily could not conceive of anything better.

Dmitry was not wealthy, in the understanding of society he was almost poor, but even this very condition increased her pleasure. In spite of everything heard and seen, in spite of the general opinion, all her mother's teachings, she, God knows why, unaccountably felt within herself that it was somehow higher and better to prefer poverty to wealth, Ivachinsky to Prince Victor. She sincerely rejoiced in her choice. It is true that she understood poverty after her own fashion, as something graceful, attractive, some new kind of ornament which would be very becoming to her; and already she impatiently constructed in her mind a strict way of life into which more money would go than into a luxurious one. She dreamed of how sweet it would be to live in poverty, to wear the simplest of dresses, sewn by Madame André, the style of which would be worth twice as much as the material itself, to furnish small rooms excellently and artfully, to ride in a light beautiful carriage, harnessed with only a pair of fine gray horses, even sometimes in good weather to walk with her husband, in a smart cloak or in a velvet coat lined with ermine. Other constraints she did not know and could not imagine. Naturally, she sometimes noticed an ugly dress or an old, clumsy carriage of another lady about whom it was said with insulting pity that she was poor; but this was indeed only ignorance, insufficiency of taste. How could it be possible not to be able to sew oneself a fashionable dress and own a decent carriage? What kind of poverty does not allow even that? It happened on her rides that she saw rotten hovels, met women in miserable threadbare clothing, who in freezing weather were covered only with an old shawl, pale men in torn overcoats, wasted children in repulsively filthy shirts; but these were inhabitants of another world, beings of another order with whom she could have nothing in common. She had before her eyes every day an example, of another, perhaps more pitiable existence, the striking example of drawing-room poverty—Nadezhda Ivanovna, and Cecily did not even think of her.

And so what was there left for her to wish for? Dmitry was passionately in love with her, Dmitry was very

85

good-looking, extraordinarily *comme il faut* and quite educated and clever. He could not appear otherwise to her. Living out her whole life in that general atmosphere of banality, she could hardly be struck by Ivachinsky's banality—just as a poor workman who never leaves his shop can hardly notice the heavy closeness of his dwelling. Besides, it isn't easy even for a woman with wider understanding to guess quickly the mediocre mind in the midst of the conventional cultivation of society. How and by what means may one in an aristocratic drawing room distinguish the vulgar man from the brilliantly intelligent one? Indeed only by the fact that here the former usually seems more clever. Finally, in addition to everything else, Dmitry was unbelievably kind and impossibly meek, even almost too meek—the distinguishing trait of all future husbands, an excess which happily disappears later on.

So, again, what more could Cecily wish for? How could she not feel herself to be a blessed creature in the world? What did she lack?

Perhaps one thing: a bit of truth among all this fine phantasmagoria. . . . But what is truth? . . .

The sun went down behind the vari-colored houses in the park. Their smart population poured out from them. Most of these suburban dwellers, these charming lovers of nature, rode along the noisy avenue to the brilliantly illuminated theatre which attracted them with a new French light comedy. The evening revived the customary daily round. Things of yesterday repeated themselves monotonously and tirelessly in the Petrovsky Park, just as they did in the heavens where against a flaming sunset a white moon arose and Arcturus glimmered, still only barely visible.

In Vera Vladimirovna's drawing room a very lively and interesting conversation was in progress. Along with a few women friends, among whom Madame Valitsky maintained first place (so skillfully and artfully had she known how to hide her brilliant match-making), Vera Vladimirovna was occupied with the chief concern of her maternal heart—Cecily's imminent wedding. She was asking for the advice of her friends about the wedding dress and the precious stones sent by the jeweller which were spread out on the table in front of her. She had to choose those that were the most becoming to the bride.

"For her wedding I gave her the best part of my own diamonds and they reworked them very tastefully," she said. "But I don't know what to decide on for the other set. Turquoise is quite unbecoming to her."

"These amethysts are very good and the work is excellent," one lady remarked. "But amethysts, however good they are, never produce an effect."

"Take opals," another lady proposed. "In my opinion they're the best stones."

"No," Madame Valitsky exclaimed, "if you wear opals, then they should be unusually fine and priced for a Tsar. I would take emeralds; they go wonderfully with black hair and fair skin like Cecily's."

"I would prefer them myself; they are indeed very good on her," Vera Vladimirovna said. "But if this is so, then I will take a set which they brought yesterday. It's incomparably better than this one. These stones are quite mediocre. They would lose a lot by comparison with Sofia Chardet's emeralds and I don't want that. Have you seen them?" she added, turning to one of those present.

"Yes," this person answered. "The young lady wore them two days ago at her aunt's evening party. They are amazingly good, especially the bracelets and buttons, and that necklace went very well with her pale yellow dress."

"She dresses beautifully," another lady said.

"Especially since she married a bag of money," added a third, smiling.

Vera Vladimirovna also smiled.

Then she said very seriously, "I can't fathom how one

can sacrifice one's daughter for money in this way. I do not believe that a mother's duty lies in acquiring a rich son-in-law. I understand it differently and more ideally. Every mother has a holy responsibility placed upon her, and she is guilty if she does not prefer her daughter's happiness to all other calculations and advantages."

"You do not merely content yourself with defining a mother's duty beautifully," Natalia Afanasevna answered her, deeply touched, "you fulfill this duty even more beautifully, a much rarer thing."

"I can at least bear witness," Very Vladimirovna continued, conscientiously and modestly, "that my words and deeds are in harmony with each other. I have always proclaimed my convictions sincerely and have always acted in keeping with them."

While these deliberations were going on, Cecily was sitting some distance away with Dmitry and listening only to his quiet words, spoken almost into her ear as if they were a secret, although there was no secret at all to them. The commonplaces which he spoke to her in this fashion could have been proclaimed anywhere at all and made known to the whole world; but all these empty speeches seemed to her, of course, interesting in the extreme. And indeed the thing that mattered was not the speeches themselves. The magnetism of a look, a smile, a voice came into play. Meaning was hidden in a thousand imperceptible circumstances. That amorous whisper, that intricate conversation were naturally prudent and proper in the highest degree. But no matter how well the young people observed the rules of good society, no matter how decorous Dmitry was, no matter how excellently educated Cecily, they still could not act like complete puppets, and between them they were hiding from Vera Vladimirovna's glance slight transgressions of society's strict laws. And all this was being done so secretly that it became a sinful act and thus all the sweeter. And what virginal soul does not understand the charm of these slight transgressions? What woman, confessing to herself, does not admit that to encourage these heartfelt, troubling joys on the sly, casually, with fear and tremor is a hundred times more intoxicating than to enjoy them in the open and tranquilly? And that we, daughters of Eve, all share more or less the opinion of that Italian countess who, eating some delicious ice cream on a torrid day, exclaimed sincerely, "Ah, what a shame that this is not a sin!"

Cecily got up from where she was sitting and went out on the balcony. Dmitry soon followed after her and they both felt almost alone. Two thick orange trees whose countless blossoms smelled sweeter toward night separated them from the drawing room and concealed them. Twilight was already closing in, distant stars began to shine brightly one after another. There were no other witnesses and Dmitry understood that under God's sky with the stars watching it was not shameful to give oneself over to his heart: he quickly clasped his lovely fiancée and pressed his lips boldly to her pale cheek. . . . She trembled, tore herself away . . . and then remained motionless, leaning against the glass door. Something had awakened in her and was glowing brighter than the stars of the night. Through all the mental shrouds, through all the ignorance, through all the falsehood of her life shone a gleam of heavenly truth, a sincere feeling, a revelation of the soul . . . a minute flowed by, perhaps unique in her earthly existence . . . and she quietly went back again into the room and sat down lost in thought.

The conversation around the table continued. Cecily listened to these words, not penetrating their meaning and answered appropriately to questions she had not understood with that strange talent which we sometimes possess or, more precisely, which possesses us in times of the heart's somnambulism. Finally all the visitors dispersed, Dmitry left too, and Vera Vladimirovna remained alone with her daughter. She used the remainder of the evening to inspect and choose fine lace with Cecily and incidentally to give her a multitude of moral lessons and useful pieces of advice. Then she made the sign of the cross over her and sent her off to bed. Cecily was impatiently awaiting this opportunity to be alone; she hastened to undress and sent the maid away.

Alone with herself she leaned her elbows on the soft pillows and submitted to her blissful reveries. An arrogant tranquility entrancingly ruled her soul. Unhappiness was a meaningless word for her. She reigned over fate. She was standing before life like a creditor before a debtor, with the right to claim his property. Boldly, without a trace of fear, she trusted in the unknown future, and in her heart, and in the heart of another. Strange, eternally new, eternally inexplicable phenomenon! What is the reason for striving so joyfully towards the unknown, for committing oneself so blindly. Where is the pledge, where is the guarantee? And that unnatural conviction, insane and always deceived, is what is right. It is the same majestic madness of Don Quixote, who orders a convoy of guards to free the convicts and deliver them to a heavenly court. He is right, the inspired madman, when he trustingly takes the chains off the criminal and only the depravity of others makes him wrong and comical.

Great souls always preserve this faith in humanity; but everyone has felt it in himself, if only for a few moments.

And they tell us as children of the deeds of Alexander the Great. Give us time, we will all, if only once in our lives, stand as an equal with him; we will all, as he did, drink from the cup, though the whole world has assured us it is poisoned.

And she continued her sweet imaginings, the happy young girl. Already her thoughts were covered in mist and her dreams wandered, confused by drowsiness; but the bliss in her soul shone through though she was half asleep. Her head bent slowly and touched the pillows . . . her eyelids closed . . . and sweetly falling asleep she suddenly shuddered as in unexpected fright; her glance shone and darkened again. And the moon came up high and looked in the window . . . and in a sudden burst, from afar, across the spaces something was carried in stormy flight, and the sleepy treetops began to rustle in the darkness, and again fell silent, scarcely breathing. . . .

All is silent; only the fountain's tears
Are falling unseen in the dark of the avenue of trees;
The leaves are sleeping, the vines do
                            not touch each other,
The quiet grows more motionless and still.

What is heard suddenly in the stillness of the night,
Quarrelling with the peacefulness?
Are the hollow depths of the sea rumbling?
Is a thunderstorm murmuring in the distance?

Whose is that nameless and mighty call?
The moon looks from on high into her eyes,
The vale is peaceful, and the heavens without clouds.
Why is her soul full of dread?

He's waiting there, where with mute shadow
The motionless cypress blackly stands:
They met with a light step,
Silently took each other's arm.

Dim understanding awakened in her,
The prophetic voice filled her heart;
And, leaning into his embrace,
Suddenly her tears poured forth.

91

Whose enlivening strength flowed
Over her among the wonders of night?
Whose thought began to speak above her,
Floating into the bottomless depths of heaven?

Was it not his? . . . Didn't her heart tremble
Like a string in mutual feeling?
Wasn't it with his euphonious song
That the fountains, and the stars and she were singing?

The time has come! . . . her soul is ready! . . . .
Come to her lips, holy sound! . . .
Crowd into a mysterious word,
A dream of all that is lofty!

Love, incomparable miracle!
How do you slip into burning hearts,
Bright guest, from a place
That has no end and no beginning?

Love, entering the corporeal world,
You are made a slave to fate,
You have no heavenly protection,
You have no help from above!

You will not smash the rules of the crowd,
You will not conquer its passions;
And you will be forever wrong,
Forever powerless before it.

A blessed dream of the earthly realm,
You will drift in the fog of life,
Known, but always foreign,
Always inaccessible to earth.

The heart will strive in vain
To embody you, holy rite.
O, cherub, flown from heaven,
You will return to heaven again!

But your soul has touched the deity,
Secrets have found tongue,
Infinity has been thrown open,
And your glance has reached into unearthly things.

They have come for a moment,
                              spirit of the universe,
Brilliant among those shining worlds,
Boundlessness into perishable form,
Heavenly light into earthly dust!

For a moment trembling souls
Are tempered in holy powers;
May eyes gaze and ears hearken,
And earthly murmurs cease!

IX

Having succeeded finally in properly arranging everything necessary for Cecily's marriage, Vera Vladimirovna set the date of the wedding. For this purpose she left the park and returned with her daughter to her house on the Tverskoi Boulevard. Meanwhile Dmitry Ivachinsky went to the country to visit his sick father in order to receive his blessing and, as much as was possible, to prepare his modest dwelling there for Cecily's arrival. She had wished to spend in rustic solitude with him those first days of marriage when newlyweds in love cannot get their fill of contemplating one another and fall into happy delusions, imagining that they have no need for the rest of the world.

Dmitry was absent for a week and in the course of that week he wrote seven long letters to Cecily. Vera Vladimirovna, through whose hands they passed, confiscated two of them. According to her strict, autocratic rules of censorship she had found in them a certain unpleasant strain of Georgesandism, which it was necessary to keep from her daughter up to the wedding itself. Perhaps she was right, but the results of her watchfulness were two sleepless nights for Cecily in which she racked her brains until morning about the possible content of these two hidden letters, tirelessly thinking up countless solutions to this interesting riddle.

Finally after this endless seven-day absence, Dmitry returned, more in love than ever. He belonged to that group of people who in all their feelings and actions seem to be walking down the steep side of a mountain. They lack the strength to stop for a minute and with each step get more and more carried along. Like all of them, Dmitry took this insufficiency of strength for fervency of character and irresistible storminess of passion. The reunion was touching. Vera Vladimirovna herself was deeply moved on this occasion and was convinced of the future happiness of her Cecily, about which the people she knew and even those she didn't know were speaking with much sympathetic interest.

The long-awaited hour drew near. On the eve of the day which was so happily to change her entire life, the bride was sitting at the window of her room and gazing in quiet contemplation at the long boulevard. It was the beginning of the second half of August, a month already nearly always autumnal in our country. The day was overcast; cold gray clouds drifted slowly across the heavens. Moscow still preserved its deserted summer appearance. Rarely did a carriage pass along the staid street. On the empty boulevard some hurried plebeian passers-by in a dark-blue kaftan or a gray peasant's coat appeared from time to time. The dusty lime-trees stood motionless with a sort of tired, bored expression. The humid air brought in rain.

What was Cecily thinking about for so long, with such a distracted look? What was the cause of this almost despondent daydreaming? She herself could not have said. We are powerless before our own incomprehensible feelings and our impressions do not depend on any external events. Who has not sometimes felt heavy and sad in his heart in the midst of a splendid holiday, of general noisy gaiety and his own happiness? Perhaps she was experiencing at that moment how strangely sometimes a person's heart fears the imminent fulfillment of his passionate wishes as if he understands, though only of an instant, all their blindness and nothingness.

The entrance of the maid Annushka interrupted this

96

wayward meditation.

"Your mother has begged to inform you that your gracious presence is requested at table; they have already sat down."

"What," Cecily said, "is it really already so late?"

"Already five o'clock, Miss Cecily."

Cecily hurried to the dining room where her mother was waiting for her.

Dmitry was not there that day.

Vera Vladimirovna wanted Cecily to spend this evening alone with her friends in something like the traditional maiden's party.

Vera Vladimirovna was well known for her patriotism and love for all Russian customs, although when she happened to observe them, she gave a rather French tone to them.

At about nine o'clock her young friends visited Cecily. Olga arrived before the others, unusually merry. Prince Victor had been extraordinarily friendly with her all these days, as she rushed to tell Cecily immediately when they were alone.

"Imagine, darling, yesterday I was in a frightful situation. You know a large cavalcade was organized near us in Pokrovskoe. That marvelous voyager whom you saw at our house, Lord Granville, took part in it and made me a bet that he would overtake me. I agreed to the bet, trusting in the speed of my horse. But that morning they suddenly came and told me that the horse was lame. This happened in the presence of Prince Victor who had dropped in to inquire about mother's health. I was in despair that I would have to refuse to take part in the cavalcade and especially that I would have to refuse the bet with my Lord. Meanwhile Prince Victor left and, imagine, an hour later he sent me his groom with Gulnara, his best horse, and he had ordered him to tell me that he sincerely wished that I would win my bet riding her. I did win indeed! How do you like that?"

Cecily shared with all her heart in Olga's happiness.

"I always thought," she said, "that you would be the wife of Prince Victor. May God grant you happiness!"

Olga threw herself into Cecily's arms. The other visitors entered and the usual conversation of young girls began: happy chatter, light mockery of absent friends, innocent secrets whispered in the ear, sometimeş by chance a caustic word—and all of this was surprisingly graceful.

Cecily of course was the Tsaritsa of the enchanted circle: her friends were paying that involuntary tribute which belongs by right to the triumphant one chosen in love. All these shrewd uninitiated Ondines understand this. She herself radiated the sweet pride that every bride feels in herself, even the betrothed of the poor tradesman. Her vague morning thoughts had completely disappeared. Once again she trusted joyfully in her fate. The young guests were busy with the presents given her by her fiancé, mother and relatives. They inspected, interrogated, praised, evaluated, envied—and the hours went by in lively fashion, gaily.

They were going by even more gaily at that same time in a room of a certain building near the Arbat gate, where Dmitry Ivachinsky lived. On that evening, conversing stormily with ten or so friends, he was bidding farewell to his bachelor's existence. Champagne was flowing, the smoke of cigars was rising around the table where dinner had ended a little while before. On the tablecloth bottles crowded thickly together, goblets sparkled and large dark spots of spilled burgundy and Chateau Lafitte appeared. The young dandies were entering an exalted state. A shout was heard, an argument, a loud laugh, sharp jokes and the whole mixture of coarse masculine pleasure. Ilichev was telling dirty jokes. His listeners were laughing at the top of their lungs. Dmitry was laughing loudest of all; he exaggerated even gaiety as well as sensitivity and sadness. He was always afraid of failing to justify to himself his respect for his own unbridled force.

Meanwhile Cecily in her circle of friends was speaking to them about the unbelievable meekness and timidity of her future husband's love and was enumerating all his virtues.

It was already quite late. The young girls went out onto the balcony. The sky was glittering, the dark clouds of the morning had gone from it and lay in a band along the horizon. Cecily leaned against the railing and remembered how she had stood with the same friends on the same balcony on a May night three months ago, and she thought with heartfelt pleasure how much had come to pass for her, how happily her fate had changed in these three months.

When all the merry guests had left, when Cecily had wished her mother good night and gone into her bedroom, she was filled with joyful agitation. In the course of the whole evening she had spoken with her friends so much about Dmitry, had so recalled and praised all his merits and fine qualities, so boasted of his love and her own happiness that, drunk with the sweet intoxication of this conversation she found herself still under the pleasant influence of her own words. She rang for the maid, freed her long braids, unwound her constricting sash, threw off her dress and her tight corset, shook off her graceful shoes with a light movement and, putting on a comfortable peignoir and soft Turkish slippers, she sent Annushka away and sat on the sofa. The door closed after the maid. Silence and peaceful twilight surrounded the young bride. The cozy bedroom was lit only by the ikon lamp, weakly and mysteriously shining from its high place. The languid ray of light fell on the bowed head with the loosened black hair, on the pure brow, on the sweet half-smile of the tender dreamer. The young soul was telling itself some silent, wonderful tale in the silence of night. The stars glimmered through the long muslin curtains on the windows of the quiet room.

In Dmitry's room the noise grew. The champagne was replaced by rum, in the middle of the table hot punch floated with a blue flame, the orgy reached its peak. Two or three of the men, weaker by nature, were already lying on the sofas, but the remaining heroes were shouting and laughing all the louder, although a bit senselessly.

"Ivachinsky!" Ilichev said drunkenly, "are you actually taking leave of the joys of life that you're drinking with such desperation?"

"I see now that you're drunk," Dmitry answered, "because you're beginning to utter absurdities."

"Gentlemen," Ilichev continued in a loud voice, raising his full glass, "I drink to Ivachinsky's health and propose a bet that from tomorrow on he'll become the most moral person and a virtuous family man. He'll take a stroll along the boulevard with his wife on his arm, drink only blameless tea, and later boiled milk with his children."

The din of laughter sounded anew.

"Do you hear that, Ivachinsky?" some voices cried out.

"I hear."

"Well, aren't you answering?"

"What should I answer to such nonsense?"

"You see, Ivachinsky," Ilichev said, "what a fine reputation you have. They all agree with me and no one wants to take up my bet."

Of all the soul's effects shame is the most relative feeling and the one most capable of distortions. Dmitry felt ashamed that these wastrels could assume him capable of settling down. Most likely in the society of brazen thieves he would have been ashamed that he did not steal.

"I'll take your bet," he cried out, "and, in a week from today, I'll invite you all to a heroic drinking bout at the gypsies'."

"Bravo!" the guests cried noisily. "It's a deal!"

"Of course," one of them added, "who would want to get married if the blessed state of matrimony made it necessary to give up wine and good times."

"He's bragging," Ilichev said. "Look at him! What if his wife were to find out!"

Dmitry waved his arm with inexpressibly heroic scorn and all at once drank his glass of hot punch to the dregs.

In her quiet bedroom Cecily was still sitting in profound meditation, but little by little her dreams were changing unaccountably. She looked around her at this modest chaste room that tomorrow she would have to leave forever, and darkly she understood much in that moment. All her childish, bright peacefulness so proudly scorned suddenly flashed before her like a priceless lost treasure. A weight lay on her heart. She tried to be comforted, enumerating to herself once again all Dmitry's virtues, all the guarantees of her future happiness, but now they somehow failed to come to her mind. More and more a senseless fear, a perplexing sadness made her soul timid. Her nerves were painfully strained. She didn't have the strength to throw off the oppressive thought from her heart. She sat with bowed head, mute under the weight of this inexplicable feeling. Suddenly a shudder ran through her and she remained motionless as in a trance. Leaning slightly forward, strangely fixing her gaze into the twilight, with inexpressible sadness on her face, through walls and through space, Cecily seemed to reach that stormy party, seemed to see the sharp flame of the hot punch and hear the piercing laughter of a well-known voice.

Finally she stood up weakly, went to the corner where the ikon gleamed in its golden frame, and fell to her knees with a heavy sigh before the holy countenance which looked so peacefully at all the heart's storms, at all earthly woe.

She lay for a long time before the ikon, trying in vain

101

to gain control of her thoughts, in bitter forgetfulness, not praying—unless grief and humility are a prayer. Then, somewhat eased, she got up, went to her bed, and lay down for the last time on that peaceful maidenly bed where for so many nights she had dreamed so sweetly, slept so quietly. Her pale forehead fell against the pillows. She lay for some time stretched out like a marble effigy on a tomb.

The fancy clock in the small column between the windows struck one sonorous chime in the silence of night. Cecily slowly raised herself up and looked. She remembered something and couldn't recall it clearly, some word which she couldn't find, some name which didn't come to her. . . . And she felt and knew for certain that all that existed now had already been with her at some time, that this minute had been repeated in her life, that she had already lived through it once. . . . "My God!" she almost whispered out loud, "who has died? . . . What is this? . . ."

She struggled with sleep.

But a timid sweetly sad feeling of expectation gradually filled her whole spirit, an indistinct desire, like another, inscrutable love. Quiet bright tears flowed from under her lowered eyelids. She fell asleep like a hurt, half-soothed child. . . . And now she remembered . . . all was mute around her. . . . Wasn't it time? . . . She was alone . . . what was going to happen? . . .

> The stars shine menacingly above her,
> The night is infinite, the valley barely visible;
> She is alone . . . perhaps it is too late,
> Perhaps, the time of encounter has passed.
>
> The midnight bird has taken wing. . . .
> The earth is silent like the grave;
> From time to time the angry summer lightning
> Flashes in the dusky distance.

And suddenly he stands beside her,
Drooping his gloomy head,
Unmoving, with a hopeless look,
In heavy, silent meditation.

"You have come again! . . . and are we
                        not in a dream? . . .
Why was our path so full of discord? . . .
Why are your lips so silent? . . .
Why does fear lie in my heart? . . ."

And he bent over, sad and pale,
And he spoke words of sadness:
"Let us say goodbye today, my poor friend:
Let life claim its rights!

Go back to the realm of earth,
Go to your earthly triumph—
I give you over to the world,
With an anxious prayer to the creator.

He has given woe to all of us,
To all a measure of sad days;
Submit to his laws
The murmur of your pride.

Learn to live with outward grief,
Forgetting youthful dreams of Eden,
Share no more with anyone
The secret of inconsolable thought.

Not in vain did your heart's longings
Tear themselves so eagerly toward reality
Life will mercilessly fulfill
Your passionate request.

And the bright glow
Of the enchanted mist will dissipate;
Too late, too soon,
You will know the gift you have awaited.

And fate will carry out to excess
Its sentence over you:
But you will not be in cruel torture,
You will not fall in battle.

You will find in the midst of struggles,
Of years illusionless and sorrowful,
Many pure attractions,
Many joyful victories.

You will bear the insults of your friends,
The evil lies of heartfelt dreams—
And you will raise the shroud
Of the mysterious goddess Isis.

You will understand earthly reality
With a maturing soul:
You will buy dear wealth
At a dear price.

You will calm the animosity in your heart,
You will not bend knowledge to misfortune,
Neither moments of deception nor of hope
Will trouble you.

All that is today unconscious
Foreign to everyone, will flower in you,—
The burning torments of life
Will turn into rich fruit

So, go as you are bid,
Strong in faith only
Not hoping for support,
Defenceless and alone.

Don't disturb the heavens, transgressing,
Silence your own dreams.
And dare to ask of God
Only for your daily bread."

X

On the following day at eight o'clock in the evening, Vera Vladimirovna's magnificently illuminated and decorated house shone in the darkening twilight. People thronged on the Tverskoi Boulevard opposite the bright windows and, as usual, admired goodheartedly the arrogant luxury and unreachable happiness of the rich. In the plush room, in front of a huge mirror lit with the bright light of candelabras, Cecily, surrounded by her young friends, was putting on that fine triumphal dress that all those pretty little heads dreamed about. The vision of it arises captivatingly and persistently in maidenly reveries; and even the poor Nadezhda Ivanovna, bustling about the bride, had still not despaired of arraying herself in it.

And the bride looked inexpressibly charming in that wedding dress, with its wonderful veil falling transparently onto her young shoulders, with those white orange blossoms trembling brightly in the black of her curls, with those sparkling diamonds, with that pale face, with those thoughtful eyes.

Cecily was feeling nervous, as is natural at such a moment, and was not able to understand her mysterious inner feelings. It seemed to her at times that she was in a dream, that they were not in fact bringing her to the church to be married, and she asked herself: how did all this come about so soon? How is it that I am marrying Dmitry?

The dressing was finished. They gave her one more rich bracelet, a gift from the groom. She stretched out her arm so they could put it on her and, looking with a distracted

107

gaze at Olga while she fastened the lock, Cecily whispered deep in thought:

So, go as you are bid,
Defenceless and alone. . . .

"What are you saying?" Olga asked, looking at her with surprise.

"I don't know," Cecily answered. "It's some song which has been turning around in my mind. I can't remember where I heard it."

"What nonsense!" Olga said. "Go on, you're ready. Put on your gloves. It's time to go."

An hour later near the Arbat gates, at the wealthy parish church of St. Nicholas, smart carriages were lining up in a long row. The church was bright with candlelight. Aristocratic society was crowded together in it and at the doors a plebeian crowd gaped at the wedding and pushed at each other jealously in order to catch a glimpse from afar of the fine couple.

Cecily stood pale with head quietly bowed beneath the heavy crown whose burden, perhaps symbolic, she seemed to feel on her young brow.* Her limbs trembled slightly and her glance flew up anxiously two or three times past the ikonostasis to the top of the cupola where a rainy sky shone black through the high windows.

Among the spectators near the doors the usual remarks, questions and answers were flying about in half whispers.

"Why is she such a serious one? Doesn't she want to marry?"

"No, it's for love."

"Look at those diamonds!"

---

*In the Orthodox wedding ceremony heavy crowns are held over (rather than placed on) the heads of the bride and groom for part of the service.

"So, then, he's rich?"

"They say he's poor."

"Well, he's good-looking."

"Tell me," a friend standing with Ilichev in the corner of the church said to him, "how come she's known as a beauty? She's not at all pretty. She's pale as a corpse."

"She's very nervous," Ilichev answered.

"Phew!" the other continued, "these nervous wives are a punishment from God! He'll be unhappy with her for life."

"He'll cure her," Ilichev said coldbloodedly.

The triumphal ceremony came to an end. Relatives, friends and acquaintances surrounded the young pair congratulating them and accompanying them to the porch of the church. At the exit, Prince Victor went up to Madame Valitsky with his haughty, barely noticeable bow.

"Can I do any errands for you in Paris?" he said to her casually. "I'm leaving for there tomorrow."

"What?" the frightened Natalia Afanasevna asked. "You are going? I hope not for long."

"I don't know," the Prince answered. "Probably for long."

Natalia Afanasevna found the strength almost to smile and utter a few words in which were included, not altogether clearly, the wish for a happy journey. The Prince bowed slightly again and disappeared along with all her fine hopes.

For what had she, poor woman, so diligently striven and so skillfully married off Cecily and Ivachinsky? All her knowledge was in vain; all her labors had come to nothing...

She bit her lips and followed the others out.

Vera Vladimirovna, standing on the porch of the church, wiped her eyes, full of tears of joy.

The carriages were brought round, the din of the wheels was heard, the clip-clop of the horses, the cry of the postilions, the shouts of the coachmen and lackeys—

109

the whole loud disturbance of departure. The crowd scattered. The lights in the church were extinguished.

Soon afterwards, the church stood dark and mute on the wide empty street. Above it heavy, menacing clouds went slowly by and were carried no one knows where.

Cherished thought claimed what was its own,
Found speech, crossed into the outer world.
Long it has lived in the midst of worldly noise,
Free and bright in me.

And long was I able in my soul
To keep it silently for myself alone,
And now I look upon my work
With an involuntary and strange sadness.

And then it occurs to me again
That it's time for me to meet life differently,
That dreams are lies, words useless,
Sounds and verses an empty game.

This is, perhaps, the final song:
Dreams fly away faster than years!
Shall I too recognize the vain power of the world?
Shall I too forget the service of beauty?

Now that my soul is warmed for the first time
Will you bid me farewell, poetry?
Will I abandon you, youthful beliefs?
Will I find a meaningless peace?

Having known the joys and sorrows of the earth,
Having lived through the anxious years,
Will I say, as many have said:
All is empty fantasy! All is sad vanity!

The spirit weakens and the goal is far-off.
The crazy hope of yesterday
Is barely remembered and the voice of self-reproach
Rings louder and more threatening in my heart.

I am weighed down with impotent striving,
I am full of heavy questions.
Consciousness alone lives in my soul,
The only strength, and may it never die!

Then let the future threaten loss,
And the heart's dreams grow thinner every day;
Let me pay a woeful price
For the bright gifts of my youth;

Let me throw treasure after treasure
Into the stormy depths of the sea of life:
Blessed is he who, arguing with the storm,
Can salvage something precious for himself.

Written between 1844 and 1847.

About the Translator

Barbara Heldt is the author of *Kozma Prutkov: The Art of Parody* and of the forthcoming *Terrible Perfection: Women and Russian Literature.* She teaches Russian literature and Women's Studies at the University of British Columbia, Vancouver.